BLACK MAMBA

J. W. Nicholas

This book is a work of fiction. Names, characters, places, organizations, and incidents are either products of the author's imagination or are used fictitiously to provide a sense of authenticity. Any resemblance to actual events, if not taken from public records, is entirely coincidental.

ISBN: 0692708820
ISBN 13: 9780692708828

Author photograph: Butch MacDonald.

A Copperthwaite Book
castle works

Also by J. W. Nicholas

The Freedom to Kill

To Joanne Trepanier

I am like a snake that has already bitten.
I retreat from a direct battle while knowing the slow effect
of the poison.

—Anaïs Nin

CONTENTS

THE MURDER

According to many sources, I have no credibility, but truth is malleable, so read carefully.

I'm a disbarred attorney, a convicted felon. I have long understood the law is anything you make it up to be. There is no math involved. Nor does good or evil exist—not until you say it does, and even then, it exists in name only. The universe doesn't care. I shared this understanding with Meyer Lacombe but little else. He's the reason I went to prison, and he's the one who freed me to do his bidding—no matter the task.

It's widely believed that Meyer Lacombe and his twin sister, Tziporah, were born in Palestine, on Kibbutz Degania Alef, within the boundary of what was once the Ottoman Empire, and they were related by blood to General Moshe Dayan. But as I have learned, it was through an act of terrorism by a Zionist paramilitary group (the Irgun) against the British—the bombing of the King David Hotel—that related them. There were only twenty original people on this kibbutz, all of whom, with the exception of six, are now deceased, so my story isn't definitive; rather it's revealed as a theory is slowly, or perhaps through sudden insight, pieced together.

The records I uncovered have since been destroyed. While in a French prison, I received an envelope addressed to me and unopened by the censors. When I opened the envelope, a tablespoon of ashes, as fine as dust, fell to the floor. I sat there, on the edge of my bunk, staring at the ashes that lay between and on my shoes. I knew at that moment I was looking at the information I had collected—evidence into fraud, murder, terrorism, and the ever-shifting identity of Meyer Lacombe. This was his way of winking at me.

The research that now dusted my shoes was initiated at the behest of my former father-in-law, Lord Nigel Firth. I was married to Adrienne Elizabeth Firth, his only daughter. She was twelve years my senior. Some might have considered her a tramp, but I don't. She was a chain smoker, addicted to amphetamines, and suffered from a severe form of premenstrual dysphoric disorder. I was twenty-two years old when I met her in a lounge atop what was once the Pontchartrain Hotel in Detroit. She sat at the bar with several women, all of whom, I later learned, were prostitutes. Adrienne got many of her pills from them, as well as the names of physicians who would prescribe anything as long as the female patient made her visit when all other patients, nurses, and technicians were gone. The premenstrual disorder left Adrienne depressed, anxious—at times near catatonic—and most certainly mean and nasty to be around for five to six days of the month. It was during those periods that she became the private prostitute for the physicians who wrote her prescriptions.

The night I met her, she had a serving tray that she'd taken from the end of the bar and was visiting patrons, laughing, joking, and asking for their orders, and she didn't even work there. The amphetamine energy would last for hours and sometimes days. When I entered the lounge, her eyes latched on to me. She looped her arm through mine, the empty serving tray under the other arm. "May I take your order, handsome?" She nudged me with her hip.

I was star-struck. Here was this beautiful woman who, through innuendo, had all but promised sex if I simply opened my mouth to talk. She had high cheekbones, a straight nose, and a chin both delicate and strong, as though all the lines of her face had been artistically drawn. Her reddish-blond hair was worn up, with long-wispy strands at the sides of her face. Her eyes were sparkling blue with flecks of hazel.

She turned to face the lounge; her arm still looped through mine, and made an announcement in her British accent, saying, "I'll have you chaps know," the amphetamines said, "I'm spoken for," and she led me toward the bar. I don't think I said more than a handful of words that night. I was infatuated…enthralled.

"What's your name?" Adrienne asked. "Please don't tell me it's Paul or Barry…anything remotely Jewish. But how could it be? Look at that face!"

"Nick," I managed to say.

"Nick," she repeated. "Nick what? No, don't tell me. It might be boring…" We were now seated at the bar. "I'll call you Nicky," she said. "I like that." She drew her head back as if to take in every angle of my appearance. "What do you do, Nicky? Please don't tell me you're an actor."

"I work in a factory," I said. "On the assembly line."

"Oh my God! Working class. Won't Father love this?" Adrienne said, looking past me to the ladies at the bar as if a myriad of secrets were shared between them. "But on looks alone," she continued, "you're an improvement over the last two—not that it'll mean anything to Father. But then, who knows? Mother claims he's queer. He divorced her, you know. So of course she has an ax to grind. Woman scorned and all that rubbish."

She crushed out a half-smoked cigarette in the ashtray and lit another one. The ashtray was filled with them, some as long as when they'd been taken from the package—lit, drawn on, smudged with lipstick, and crushed out.

"Of course, we'll have to educate you," she said.

The young man behind the bar refilled her glass without being asked. The young prostitutes at the bar drank for free in exchange for oral sex. Adrienne he viewed differently. She was out of his league.

"We'll teach you how to speak," she continued. "Properly, that is. Are you table trained?" She read my expression. "Manners, handsome—how are your table manners? You don't use the wrong fork, do you? Oh God!" She rolled her eyes. "Of course, we'll teach you what *not* to say. That will impress Mother. She likes them obedient. I warn you, she's quite the bitch." She crushed the cigarette out and then looked at me as though a thought had occurred to her.

"We'll send you to law school. That's it! Father will love that. Makes one useful, you know—the law. Butch never was. Father despises him. Says he's useless. He's quite right, you know. Even in bed...useless."

When she referred to the "last two," she didn't mention—not then anyway—that she was still married to number two, Clyde Truxkle of Detroit Diesel & Design. But Clyde didn't like his name, and in keeping with children who don't like their parents for some imagined or actual slight of affection, he changed his name in a show of defiance, the verisimilitude of independence. With boys it tends to be the catchall of nicknames, "Butch." I once asked Adrienne why she had married him, and as the amphetamines and alcohol left her system, she answered in an evasive, even shy manner. It was money, she admitted, enough to escape her parents, especially her mother, who belittled her for daring to ask for love and who was jealous of Adrienne's closeness to her father, and, as I later learned, *very jealous.*

Adrienne had been raised from birth by nurses, nannies, and boarding schools. Butch's boorish, uneducated presence was icing on the cake in Adrienne's silent war against her mother. Just the sight of Butch made her mother squirm with shame.

Fillmore Truxkle was the founder, the genius behind Detroit Diesel & Design, while his loutish son was devoid of any business sense, or common sense, according to Adrienne's father, Nigel. But in all fairness, I never met Clyde Truxkle. I heard of his antics through Adrienne and read of his failures in the newspapers. When Fillmore passed away, Detroit Diesel & Design went into the hands of Clyde Truxkle. Within five years the company went into bankruptcy, and Clyde invested his last dollars in a fishing enterprise off the coast of the Florida Panhandle. (From diesel design to fish—that must have been a red flag for any investor.) Shortly thereafter the fishing enterprise went into bankruptcy, and Adrienne was back in Detroit, living with a girlfriend who worked as a lounge waitress whom she had met through a need to beg amphetamines. At this point Adrienne's parents had no idea where she was or whether she was even alive.

Adrienne never filed for divorce; Clyde Truxkle did. He filed on the basis of desertion. A week after I'd met Adrienne, she and I ran off to Chicago. It was the summer of 1968. We had ninety dollars between us. We found a hotel room with a pull-down bed, a closet-size kitchen, and a distant view of Lake Michigan. At a weekly rate of eighteen dollars, the room was cheap. The neighborhood was made up of East European immigrants and a few Mexicans. Beneath the elevated train tracks were small shops and stalls tended to by Poles and Lithuanians. Adrienne worked at Goldblatt's Department Store, and I got a job at Motorola. I was given a written test, and I did so well on it that I was practically a celebrity at the company. Executives would stop and look at me as if puzzled and then continue down the hall, glancing over their shoulders.

I was placed in the purchasing department, and a few weeks later, I was moved to legal. At first I was confused by all the attention my test score delivered. I always had thought of myself as a slow learner, although in time I've added the caveat: when I finally get it, *I get it*.

The first month I lived with Adrienne, I was introduced to premenstrual dysphoric disorder. For years I thought her behavior was a rejection of me; this Jekyll-and-Hyde creature seemed to come from nowhere. She might sit on the floor in a dark closet for hours, cry for no reason, burst into anger, throw things—ashtrays, coffee cups—or stand with her face pressed against a wall, makeup running down her cheeks, and murmur, "Soon I'll disappear. Soon I'll disappear..." Or I might find her squeezed into the storage space beneath the kitchen sink like a child frightened by gargoyles. When I first saw this behavior, I thought it was an act, an affectation, but the hormonal nightmare was real. She spoke of suicide as though it were a friend she were waiting to meet—or a blind date.

During these periods she would do anything for a handful of pills—narcotics, barbiturates, anything that might offer an escape from the depression and hopelessness that had become her torment. She once admitted to picking through her own feces in a desperate search for a remnant of a pill that might have made it through with some magic still left in it. By the second day of her menstrual cycle, as if she had stepped out of the darkened closet, a different Adrienne would appear, a more normal woman; although, for Adrienne, normal was an ethereal state.

While at Goldblatt's, Adrienne worked for the buyer of furnishings, Herman Rosenblatt. When I first heard this, I hoped she had kept her anti-Semitism sheathed or, more preferably, checked at the door. But in a short time, she spoke of Mr. Rosenblatt in a warm, affectionate manner. That fall Adrienne had become pregnant, and it was beginning to show. Herman Rosenblatt couldn't have been more fatherly, whether she had been his own daughter or not. He was concerned as to how long she was on her feet, always offering a chair, telling the other girls to be more considerate, to help ease the load for the young mother-to-be. Each day he brought Adrienne's lunch, prepared by his wife from old Jewish recipes—long tested, he said, to provide health and love to mother and child. This Jew, with a mere fringe of gray hair on along his temples, protruding lips, thick glasses, and no more than five foot five, offered the love of a parent the likes of which Adrienne had never known before. For years to come, she spoke of him with affection, as she spoke of her nurse, the woman who had cared for her from birth to puberty and who had one day suddenly disappeared—at her mother's direction—leaving an emotional hole in Adrienne's heart that never went away.

In all honesty I don't know how I fit into Adrienne's life—not emotionally, anyway. I was practically a child when she decided she wanted me, and as my education progressed, at her encouragement, I grew apart from her as one leaves a parent to enter the world in front of them. Unaware.

There is little known of Meyer and Tziporah's time at the kibbutz. Of the stories that are repeated, their accuracy may exist in paraphrase, but in the retelling from one person to another, there seems to be a consistency.

Rachel Yuksek, the mother of Meyer and Tziporah, arrived in Palestine several months pregnant. Her complexion was olive, her hair black, her eyes crystal dark, her profile Persian and regal. She had journeyed alone from a small village in Turkey. She said her husband had been killed in a pogrom outside Izmir. Some members of the commune thought the story was made up to give legitimacy to the unborn child, while others, who had suffered as she had, or who had relatives who had suffered the same, believed her.

On a late December night, Rachel Yuksek went into labor. Three midwives were in attendance through the delivery. The first child was a girl, and then a second child emerged, a male. This was proof that Rachel's story was true; she did, in fact, see her husband killed. Right in front of her eyes—for if a woman witnesses the death of her husband, she'll give birth to twins. "It is through God's consent," the midwives whispered among themselves.

The eldest of the midwives told the story throughout the commune, and the other women, upon hearing this, said, "Yes, this is certainly true." And the men, in solemn agreement, nodded and said, "It is *certainly* God's way."

Although Rachel's story was now believed to be true, a few women of the commune were reserved in their acceptance of her. Behind Rachel's dark crystal-like eyes lay her true past, and the women sensed this; and behind Rachel's silence was the true nature that gave birth to these strange twins.

The infants were wrapped together, naked in the same blanket, for warmth against the cold. Rachel held them to her breasts as they faced each other, each infant with a nipple.

Here is the first mention of the future General Moshe Dayan. It is said that he appeared at the door while Rachel nursed the twins. She called to him, "Come here."

Moshe was the first child born at the kibbutz, and because of this, he was seen as an amulet, an omen of good for the future of Jews. He was fifteen at the time, well into puberty. The sight of this woman's breasts, full and large, made him turn red and look away, yet a desire at the pit of his young manhood made his heart race. Rachel called him forward to place a hand on each infant. Her voice didn't have the placation of a female but rather some unseen authority. Moshe was too young to understand the power—the power of a firstborn—that he seemed to have over the elders. He simply did as he was told. Not until years later—before Meyer had slipped from one identity to another—did the fate of this touch come to fruition outside the King David Hotel in Jerusalem.

At the age of five, the twins lost their mother. The commune had grown to thirty-five adults, but that winter a virulent strain of influenza claimed seven of the group. Rachel Yuksek was the first to pass away. She had lain for days in a sweaty fever, dehydrated and delirious. Meyer and Tziporah were at their mother's bedside when she died. They didn't attempt to touch her or speak to her but looked at each other when their mother had stopped breathing—as though their silence were a language only they understood.

The twins became orphans of the community. From the very beginning, they were seen as inseparable. When, for some reason, they were separated from each other, they became agitated and mean toward the other children until they were reunited. They shared food with each other, and in the rare instance when a form of candy came into their possession, they seemed to take pleasure in sharing it with each other as one might present a gift to a lover.

This was about the time Ayla Shvenek arrived at the kibbutz with a three-month-old infant. She had traveled from Rome to Brindisi with a tiny bundle of clothes, a hairbrush, a toothbrush, a bar of soap, twenty liras, and her infant daughter at her breast. From Brindisi to Palestine, she'd traveled on a merchant ship. For ten liras she had received a place to hide and one meal a day. The man who delivered her meal, and who had provided her hideaway, made it clear he expected certain "favors" in return. The old woman who related this story to me said of Ayla, "Chutzpah. That's what it took! Think of it."

While in Rome, Ayla had trained as a nurse and had twice been sent to the Vatican. Her Jewish blood was hidden behind blue eyes and curly red hair. While in attendance of a young man of the Swiss Guard, she'd become pregnant. He denied knowing Ayla, saying she was obviously a tramp looking for someone to support her bastard. The women of the commune were suspicious of Ayla. They were convinced her child was a bastard; she was, therefore, the most suitable guardian for the secretive twins.

The twins never took to Ayla, but they obeyed her. Ayla never made demands of them. She never ordered them about. They simply could follow her example or not.

At age ten Meyer became ill. He suffered a fever and swelling under his jaw and around his neck and throat, and as Ayla discovered while changing the bedclothes, his testicles also were swollen. The fever persisted, and the swollen glands were red and sore to the touch. Ayla asked Tziporah not to remain so close to her brother, as she believed his illness was contagious. But once banished from the sickroom, Tziporah would later find a way to return. She was once seen hiding under the bed while Ayla was attending to young Meyer.

As they grew older, the bond between Meyer and Tziporah grew even stronger and not simply as a product of need or emotion but something deeply genetic, as if they were a single life-form. This was also the time when Ayla departed from their lives. A man had stopped at the commune with an injured foot; he was a carpenter from Nazareth. Ayla saw to the wound and cared for him until his foot was healed. When he was ready to travel, Ayla left with him. The twins, it was later said, didn't seem to notice she was gone.

Once they were into puberty, Meyer and Tziporah were observed more than once bathing naked together in the moonlight in a stream near the Sea of Galilee. When a communal elder brought this, and several other such incidents, to the kibbutz's attention—the impropriety of it—Tziporah reacted as a mountain lioness might behave with sheathed aggression. On the surface Meyer behaved with calm. But his reaction to threats, veiled or otherwise, was as certain as death—as it was toward Khayyam Rashad.

Khayyam was twenty years older than Tziporah. Her adolescent, gypsy-like beauty and voluptuous figure caught his attention as a crimson rose might captivate, with the ability to bloom in the moonlight. His suggestive comments turned to touching, and her annoyance turned to anger, yet he persisted. She felt his hand grope her full buttocks, and as she turned, in full swing, her fingernails cut like razors across his cheek. In reaction, and with a speed much younger than his years, he struck her. Her head snapped back, and blood appeared from her bottom lip. Meyer was only a few feet away. He quickly took Tziporah by the arm to help her to her feet, and in a state of calm certitude, he looked Khayyam in the eyes but said nothing. Khayyam sneered and looked around at the others who had been watching, or waiting perhaps, for Meyer to react, to see a fight, but there was nothing. Three days later Khayyam Rashad was found in the very stream where Meyer and Tziporah had bathed, his throat cut from one side to the other, nearly decapitated. Tziporah later was seen washing blood from Meyer's trousers. Meyer had been bitten, Tziporah explained to inquiring eyes, by a wild dog.

The next record of Meyer and Tziporah appears in Alexandria, Egypt. He and Tziporah were in their early twenties at this point, when Meyer married Samira Khashi, the widowed sister-in-law of Hussein bin Ali, a cousin within the House of Saud. Meyer's transition from Jew to Muslim was seamless and unquestioned, as was his assimilation from vagabond to patrician. This puzzled me until I realized there's no difference between the two, Jew or Arab, or, for that matter, from desert nomad to tribal leader. They're of the same family, and their differences are a family feud, an incestuous battle that might well end in self-destruction for both. Meyer's true allegiance was revealed much later. But for now he and Tziporah claimed whichever tribal connection suited their need, and their need was to survive at any cost, Jew or Muslim, and to prosper.

The marriage of Meyer Lacombe and Samira Khashi was arranged by Hussein bin Ali, the oldest and only surviving direct male family member after years of tribal conflict. Meyer had brokered a minimal arms deal between a British black marketer and bin Ali. The black marketer had been dealing with the Zionists of Palestine, with whom Meyer had been familiar since his early years, and the bombing of the King David Hotel.

The firstborn of this marriage between Meyer and Samira was to be looked upon as a bond for the future, but no child came. It was thought Samira was barren. There was no other answer. But Meyer and Tziporah learned the truth through intuition and experience. A nearly life-threatening case of mumps had left Meyer infertile.

Samira, thinking she was useless as a woman, became overly jealous and nasty toward Tziporah. She said Tziporah was smothering Meyer and even suggested Tziporah's covert affection for her brother was unnatural, obscene; Samira had once seen from her hiding place a kiss between Meyer and Tziporah, on the mouth, and she now foolishly threw this in Tziporah's face. Samira's jealousy was reason enough for Tziporah to do away with this sniveling creature. The nature of the relationship between brother and sister was never openly acknowledged, but their blind loyalty to each other was an adumbration with its own shadow. Not until much later, when Tziporah married John Savensworth for the same reasons of business that Meyer had married into the House of Saud, did the suspicions of the family begin to arise, and now Samira was adding jealous "speculation" to the whispered rumors.

Not until Meyer was well established in his brother-in-law's import-export business (the front for a fledgling arms trade) did the marriage between Meyer and Samira end. While on Mediterranean holiday, Samira fell from the bow of the family yacht. Tziporah and Samira, along with servants and crew members, were the only occupants aboard. Tziporah reported that Samira surfaced only once and then disappeared beneath the water. The body never was recovered. A trail of blood was seen in the water and then dissolved as a ribbon of smoke dissipates in the air. The probability that she had been eaten by sharks was unlikely, yet folklore and superstition prevailed. Tziporah was supposedly the only witness to the event, but there was one other witness who claimed to have seen the accident from a concealed portion of the bridge, a servant. This servant knew that if he contradicted Tziporah's story in the least, his own life would end. In the years that followed, this servant, Mohammed Algenib, became devoted and unquestionably loyal to Tziporah, and she concealed his preference for his own sex from the Muslim world.

News of the tragic accident was radioed ashore, and Meyer was soon at the dock to meet Tziporah. According to the crew members, Meyer appeared far more concerned with Tziporah than the sudden loss of his wife. It was observed that he noticed a small amount of blood on Tziporah's white scarf and that she had remarked that perhaps she had cut herself and then quickly gave her attention to Meyer. She kissed him on the cheek, and as they turned to leave, according to one witness, there was a sparkle in Tziporah's eyes—the glint of dark crystal.

⊫⊣⊢⊨

Adrienne and I were in Philadelphia at this time. Meyer and Tziporah were completely unknown to me, and our horrific meeting was still years in the future.

It was spring, and I was watching a Mets game on TV in the waiting room of the maternity ward at Bryn Mawr Hospital. Adrienne was six months pregnant when we left Chicago. She didn't like the Midwest; she preferred the East Coast and Philadelphia in particular. As a younger woman, she had attended Bryn Mawr College.

Graham was born in the spring. I was very proud of him, this blond, blue-eyed child, whom I held up as if to say, "Look at what I produced!" Yet *I* was still a child, and now I had the responsibility of raising a child. I had no idea how to go about it, but such questions never occurred to me. You simply go forward, and life happens to you: tomorrow is as vague as "once upon a time."

When I admitted to Adrienne that I had never finished high school, her campaign was on. "How will you ever meet my father?" she asked. "Or earn a living, for that matter?"

"I did well enough at Motorola."

"You were lucky."

"That was it? Just luck?" I wasn't looking for a compliment or a retraction; my question was rhetorical.

"No," she said. "You *are* smart. Bloody smart. But you need it on paper, to show those who aren't."

I liked hearing someone say I was smart, but with all my heart, I didn't believe it. I might as well have been a vampire looking for my image in a mirror.

I wasn't about to attend night school (I had an aversion to it), so I bought a book to prepare for the GED. The book was huge and covered science, language, math, and everything in-between. I loved it. I would lie on the floor with Graham near me and read one page after another, through each section and back again, not because I was trying to "study" but because I found it so interesting, and with little or no effort, the material stuck. Adrienne would quiz me from one topic to another, and the answers were always at the front of my mind, like friends, playmates, companions for life.

"That's amazing," she said. "You got every bloody one."

I took my GED test at Temple University, and within a few weeks, I received a brown envelope from the state. I opened it to an excellent score. That fall I enrolled at Philadelphia Community College, and two years later, I transferred to the University of Pennsylvania. I applied for financial aid, but tuition and living expenses came from a surprising source. Adrienne was an heiress of sorts. The Copperthwaite Mining & Mineral Company of South Africa was in the family, and her great-grandmother still resided in Durban, South Africa. At some point she and Adrienne had started corresponding, and large checks began to arrive on birthdays, anniversaries, and Christmas. This might have been the most perfect time of my life. I found academia to be a wonderful environment—the people, the books, the stimulation, and the intellectual attention were almost sexual in their pleasure.

Although Adrienne was getting older, menopause was certainly nowhere in sight, and her Jekyll-and-Hyde condition still arrived every month and was still just as dark. While she was pregnant, she didn't drink or take pills. Graham was three years old, almost four, when her past behaviors revisited us in force. At first I thought it simply was irritableness, but then she would go on cleaning binges, removing clean clothes from the dresser, rewashing and ironing them, and putting them neatly back in the drawer, perfectly folded. Then she would clean the bathroom, the kitchen, the bedroom, and living room and scrub the front porch. She sometimes cleaned every room twice. Her energy went on for hours, and then the crash would arrive, the darkness, the melancholy, the depression, the near-catatonic hours spent in a closet. Her eye makeup smeared and runny, she'd smoke one cigarette after another. If I had been older, not a child myself, I might have seen this as an illness, not a rejection of me or something I'd done. To make matters worse, I retreated into my newfound intellectual world with new friends and interests. To have coffee and discuss poetry and ideas with sweet young females from campus provided an escape into abundant sex. But when an unpaid parking ticket arrived in the mail, I was pulled back to reality, which, although unintended, produced an epiphany that one day saved my life, while at the same time sent Tziporah on a life-ending quest to inflict punishment in her own fashion.

The parking ticket was issued on Baltimore Avenue in what was once a working-class section of Philadelphia but had since decayed into an area of ethnic transients with escalating crime. On a few occasions, I had driven through the section, but I never stopped there, never parked on Baltimore Avenue.

"I'm not going to pay it," I told Adrienne. "I'll go to court. I've never been there. Look at the address!"

She offered nothing—neither protest nor encouragement.

When I arrived at traffic court, I was armed with my innocence. The court would admit the mistake, and that would end it. I was seated in the first row behind the railing and watched the proceedings at the bench. The judge was an older man with yellowish-gray hair, thinning and uncombed. His look alone was surly. The man pleading his case before the bench was perhaps the same age as the judge, but his hair didn't have the same dirty-yellowish tinge.

"I have three witnesses," the man said. He removed three letters from a manila envelope and set them on the bench in front of the judge. "They're notarized." He pointed to the seals on the letters. "All three swear I stopped at the stop sign—a complete stop."

The man was still pointing at the letters, when the judge pushed them from his bench with an angry swipe of his hand. "I don't give a crap," he said as the letters were pushed from the bench, oscillating to the floor. The judge banged his gavel. "Pay the fine or go to jail." He pointed toward the bailiff with the gavel.

"But—"

"One more word and I'll hold you in contempt." He slammed the gavel again.

The man shuffled toward the bailiff as if his tail, now between his legs, were in his way.

There were three more cases before me, and I watched them closely. I listened; I observed the unspoken. Then it was my turn. I approached the bench with the same feeling I'd had when I'd first realized, only a few years earlier, that going to the doctor doesn't cure you. What you get is the doctor's interpretation of what you're telling him, and his advice, and perhaps a medication to ameliorate your symptoms. He doesn't provide a cure; he has none.

As I came forward, the surly old man behind the bench looked at me over the top of his glasses. "Who are you?" he said, looking at a piece of paper in front of him.

Somehow it didn't sound like a question, so I said nothing.

"Why are you here?" he asked. "You just going to stand there?"

"The date on this ticket…" I said. "I wasn't on Baltimore Avenue then. I wasn't even in the neighborhood. It's a mistake."

He looked at the copy of the ticket in front of him. "What model do you have?"

"Model?"

"What *kind* of car?"

"Ford."

"Color?"

"Red."

"Pay the fine!" He slammed the gavel and pointed it toward the bailiff.

I made no protest. This was the first installment on my legal education. The law is written out on paper, codified in black and white, but it has no definition. The meaning of the law is subjective, and to plead it successfully, to use it to your advantage, requires creativity, for the law is not black and white as the ink used to create it. Rather it's a myriad of colors to create an illusion—the bidding of others.

By the time I was out of the courthouse and in the public parking lot and in my car, I realized the truth behind the parking ticket. Adrienne had gotten it. She'd been in the Baltimore Avenue neighborhood to find a doctor to write a prescription for the drugs she was again using.

From Samira's dowry and with the blessing of Hussein bin Ali, Meyer established Navigation Enterprises, a successful shipping company that used roll-on, roll-off ferries. But the political actions of President Gamal Abdel Nasser, nationalizing all "substantial" private companies, forced Meyer to leave Alexandria or lose control of his company. He and Tziporah soon took up residence in England, in London's Park Lane Hotel, and within a year he reestablished Navigation Enterprises in Genoa, Italy.

The shipping industry was always a mainstay for Meyer, but he also diversified. Within the Middle Eastern mind-set, I suppose, there's always the thought of oil, and this led Meyer to Haiti, to a brief business relationship with Papa Doc Duvalier.

Under the advice of Russian ex-patriot and petroleum geologist George de Mohrenschildt, friend to Jacqueline Bouvier Kennedy, Meyer undertook the development of the Lacombe-Duvalier refinery. The idea of finding oil in Haiti might seem ill conceived, since previous attempts in the Dominican Republic had come out negative. But from all witnesses, it seems Mohrenschildt was so taken with Tziporah that he would have looked for oil on the moon if it put him in her company. Meyer was far less jealous of Mohrenschildt's attention toward Tziporah than he was irritated. At this point Meyer was a confident, handsome young man with raven-black hair, deep-set eyes, and a profile that was the silhouette of Persian nobility. Tziporah worked her charm toward Meyer's goal of a refinery on the island of Haiti. She smiled and kept Mohrenschildt entertained, although at a distance, she thought.

While in Haiti, Meyer, Tziporah, and Papa Doc Duvalier were introduced to a friend of George de Mohrenschildt, who had arrived from Havana by private aircraft. The five of them had their picture taken on the grounds of the presidential mansion. In the photograph the man identified as Lee Harvey Oswald was seen showing Meyer the bolt-action mechanism on a Carcano rifle. How Oswald and Mohrenschildt had become friends, or the nature of their relationship, was of little concern to Meyer. He was more interested in Mohrenschildt's relationship to the Bouvier family and their ties to the family behind Standard Oil. But when the test results revealed that Haitian oil was nothing more than low-grade molasses, Meyer terminated his stay in Haiti.

Mohrenschildt followed the twins to London and continued his pursuit of Tziporah until one evening when she slapped him in the face at a dinner party in front of many people. A few days later, Tziporah was arrested. Mohrenschildt claimed she had stolen personal papers and jewelry from his safe, but the charges were soon dropped. On Tziporah's behalf, Meyer sued on the grounds of false arrest but lost the suit. Within a year, although he'd never attended law school, Meyer had gathered an extraordinary pool of legal talent; expertise in English, French, and international law was now under his control. He was building an empire according to "law." The firm was internationally known as Lacombe & Lacombe.

Adrienne was insistent that I got to law school. I wasn't opposed to the idea, but I had thoughts of science, such as physics and astronomy. To look up into the night sky, the endlessness of space, gave pleasure to my curiosity. Adrienne rolled her eyes, crushed out her cigarette, and led me by the hand to the other room, as her free hand went under her skirt to remove her panties as we walked. "Come with me," she said. "We'll talk about it."

I sent out several applications, the first of which was to Detroit Mercy School of Law, but the University of Pennsylvania was the first to respond, and I was accepted. Days later I was also accepted at Detroit Mercy.

"We are not going to Detroit," Adrienne said. "A greasy factory town!" She picked up the letter from the University of Pennsylvania, read a few lines, and set it back down. "My grandmother is paying," she said, pushing the letter in front of me. "And we won't have to move."

Law school was intimidating until I realized almost everyone believed the law to be an objective force. In an open discussion with faculty and students, I heard myself say, "The law is anything you make it up to be." I said this with innocent amusement. "This is not physics," I said. "There's no math involved."

For a moment there was an uncomfortable silence, and then a female professor said, "I believe you're talking about esoteric control?" She moved to the center of the room. Her hair was almost strawberry in color, full of curls, and frizzy. She wore tight jeans and leather boots that reached above her knees—a fantasy of pirate sex. The young male students couldn't take their eyes off her.

She looked at me with a white smile and ocean-green eyes. "You see the law as a form of control. Without fairness. Simply an exercise of power. Correct?"

Her name was Evelyn Gordon. She was a Jew with ancestral roots in Northern Europe and was teaching at Penn on a provisional contract. I'd seen her several times before on campus, but I'd never spoken to her. As far as I knew, I was invisible to her.

"I can see your thoughts," she said. "What is fair and what is unfair is totally subjective to you. Am I right?"

She was right, but I didn't say anything. After the discussion, as everyone started to disperse, she approached me and suggested we have coffee and discuss my thoughts. I didn't answer, not immediately; I was intimidated by her sudden attention.

"Well?" She looked at me. "I'm not going to twist your arm."

"Yes," I said. "Yes, of course, I'd love to."

We stopped at her office to drop off a few things. There was a color photograph of two young girls, perhaps eight and ten years old, on her desk. On a bookshelf in the back of her desk was another photograph. An older couple, looped arm in arm, smiling, almost giggling into the camera. The woman, perhaps in her late sixties, also had red frizzy hair and a white smile.

"Where was this taken?" I asked. "Upstate New York?"

"No," Evelyn said, turning off the overhead lights. "France, actually. Meaux. Have you been there?"

"No. I've never been out of the country."

"You have a passport?"

"No."

"Then how will you visit me?" She laughed. "But first we'll have coffee."

We had coffee at an outdoor café on campus. It was mid-April, and the flowering dogwoods perfumed the humid air. The petals lay large and slippery on the ground.

"My parents visited one summer," she said, speaking of France, "and never left."

"They still live there?"

"They bought a house. Just outside Meaux."

"What about your husband? What does he do?"

"He's a French national. A lawyer. He works in Paris. We don't see much of each other."

I nodded; the meaning was simple.

"Believe me," Evelyn said, perhaps reading my silence, "it's quite cliché. He lives his life, and I live mine…Quite boring, really—the story, I mean."

"And you work here?"

"Yes, but I spend the summer in Meaux. You should visit sometime." There was a slight sparkle in her eyes, and I knew that somehow I would make it happen.

Adrienne's Jekyll-and-Hyde condition had become worse because of her dependence on drugs. She used drugs to get through the hard part, but once the drugs started to leave her system, she suffered withdrawal, which was another form of her condition. Had I been older, I might have reacted differently, but I'd just turned thirty, so in the scheme of things, I was still a child—Adrienne's child.

But the days when Adrienne and I had anything in common had become so few that it seemed I was deceiving a stranger when I first cheated on her. I came home one night smelling of French perfume. Adrienne knew exactly what had happened. She screamed and smashed a few things, but her heart wasn't in it. The inevitable was facing her. I was no longer the young kid she had picked out of the Detroit rubble. The child she had hoped to raise was disappearing.

In early June I devised a sloppy story to explain my absences for a week or so. I was going to New Orleans for a legal seminar. I created a theme and a guest speaker, Dr. Amon. Adrienne accepted it not so much with anger but amusement at my amateur attempt to pull off what she had perfected in her past marriages. We both knew I would be back.

I boarded an Air France flight from Philadelphia International Airport. I was in the air most of the night. I drank wine, ate cheese, and thought how debonair I was in my transatlantic tryst.

I boarded a train from Charles de Gaulle Airport to Meaux. I didn't realize the train went first to Paris and then west to Meaux, but I was so enthralled with the sights and the thought of all the history that I could have been all day on the train and loved it.

At the Meaux train station, I called Evelyn from a public phone. At first I fumbled with the coins to get them in phone.

The phone rang several times, and then Evelyn answered. She laughed when she heard it was me. "You actually came," she said. "Wonderful! I'll be there shortly."

She showed up in an old Ford station wagon, a Woodie that could have been used by the Beach Boys in California. I threw my bag in the back of the wagon and got in the front seat next to her. She looked at me with both hands on the steering wheel and smiled. "You're so damn cute," she said. "But you know that, don't you?" She turned the ignition to start the car, looked at me again, then turned her eyes back to the road. "How about a glass of wine?" she asked.

She drove across the La Marne River and stopped at a café near the university. She ordered wine and sandwiches of melted cheese on crusty bread with slices of tomato and mushroom. The wine was dark red with the spicy taste of chocolate and cherry. Evelyn bit into her sandwich, and the white cheese stretched out like a long rubber band, without breaking, as she pulled the slice from her mouth. She caught the stringy cheese on her finger, twisted it, and put it in her mouth. She held her finger in her mouth as she looked up at me.

"What do you think so far?" she said, licking the end of her finger.

"I love it. The train ride was wonderful."

"We'll take the train into Paris—maybe next week."

"Next week?"

"How long are you staying?"

"My return flight leaves next week," I told her.

"We can change that. It's no problem."

My first thought was of the continuing lies I'd have to tell Adrienne, but I soon forgot that.

When we arrived at the house, I learned that I'd stay in the guest cottage with Evelyn and that the closets still contained her husband's clothes. In the dresser was his underwear, and on the bookshelves his many law books. Her two daughters were in the main house with their grandparents, but it seemed that every time I had my hands on Evelyn, one of them arrived through a doorway. The fact that a strange man had his hands on their mother's butt, or was kissing her, didn't bother them. It was obviously a sight they'd seen before.

That afternoon in the bedroom, with the curtains fully open and the room filled with light, she unbuttoned the front of my shirt while kissing my face.

"Why so tense?" she asked softly, her lips touching my nose.

"It's so strange. Your husband's stuff is still here. I thought you lived apart...?"

"Where else would he leave it?" She pulled her blouse over the top of her head. While she was in Europe, she didn't use deodorant or shave her underarms. It first appeared as red stubble, and when she was aroused, her scent was like spiced wine.

By the third day I was comfortable with her daughters coming in and out any time of day; one morning while we were still asleep, they bounced onto the bed to wake us. But the thought of her husband suddenly showing up unannounced didn't put me at ease. Would he too, one morning, simply bounce onto the bed?

Her parents were a delight. Her mother's red hair was streaked with gray and frizzy like her daughter's. She was forever smiling and seemed to be a genuinely happy soul. Her father was a retired economics professor from Rutgers University, who spoke incessantly of the need for a strong Israel. "What would the world do," he asked, "if the Arabs obtain nuclear weapons? Think about it."

"I prefer not to," his wife said.

"Well, you must, my dear."

"I agree with Daddy," Evelyn said.

"The very ground you stand on," her father continued, "once bore the boots of the Gestapo. Think about it."

Evelyn peeled the skin from a juicy peach and held it up to my mouth to bite into. The juice ran down my chin.

It was on the fifth day of my stay when the inevitable happened. Her husband appeared early in the morning. I heard voices in the kitchen as I got out of bed. I came through the hallway and through the kitchen entry. We stared at each other. He was tall, with sandy blond hair, gray eyes, and a slight smile that was nearly a smirk, as if he alone understood human behavior and found it amusing.

Evelyn looked at me. She wore a long see-through blouse to mid-thigh. She was naked underneath. "Nick," she said, "this is Marcel." She looked toward Marcel. "Nick is a student of mine."

He said something to her in French, and she replied sharply, "*Ne soyez pas un âne futé. Et pourquoi êtes-vous ici?*"

"Since you are so kind to ask," he said with sarcasm, "I thought I could be your guide through Paris." He looked at me. "Nicky, you would like to see Paris, no? The histories?"

This didn't feel right, and the insult of referring to me as "Nicky" was certainly no sleight of hand.

"*J'ai une affaire pour toi,*" Evelyn said to him. "You drive us into Paris, buy our lunch, and we'll take the train back."

When Evelyn and I were alone, she said the girls had told their father on the phone that I was there. "It seems you've made quite an impression on them. Marcel is jealous."

At that point I remembered that I too was a father, and Graham was without me. Had I been older, I might have felt a sense of shame, as I do now, but young people are often without shame and unaware of their behavior.

The drive into Paris was tense. Marcel insisted that I sit in the front seat. Evelyn sat in the back, in the middle, as if to have an equal view of us both. No one said much of anything.

Once we were in Paris, we came upon a construction site or, more accurately, the renovation of an older hotel, Hôtel Ritz. "Simply put," Evelyn said, "a luxury hotel."

The notice in front of the building gave details about the renovation, the financing, and new ownership.

"That's odd," Evelyn said.

"What is?" Marcel said.

"It says Navigation Enterprises is financing it."

"So?"

"I thought Meyer Lacombe bought the hotel."

"He did."

"Lacombe is a Jew. Why is an Egyptian financing it?"

"Lacombe *is* Egyptian."

"No, he isn't! I've met his sister. They're Jews, like us."

"*Tu ne sais pas de quoi tu parles.*"

"I *do know* what I'm talking about!" she snapped.

"I work closely with the law firm Lacombe & Lacombe. He's an Arab. His wife was Saudi."

I looked back at Evelyn; she rolled her eyes and didn't mention it again. But she did seem off in thought, as though she were still thinking about it.

"Before lunch," Marcel said, "I have something to show your student." He glanced at me.

"What now?" Evelyn said with irritation.

"A point of interest," he said. "A history—Forty-Two Rue de la Santé."

It seemed Evelyn wasn't familiar with the address because when we arrived, she seemed surprised and then upset. From inside the parked car, I looked out at the building in front of me. There was something vaguely familiar in its construction.

"La Santé Prison," Marcel said. "The oldest in Paris. It still keeps a guillotine. Interesting, no?"

It was built in the same manner and style as Eastern State Penitentiary in Philadelphia. I'd once toured the prison and went through the cell that had held Al Capone. The prison was laid out in the design of spokes extending from a hub. At the time I thought the old prison interesting, even romantic, as history holds romance, and now I was looking at its sister prison.

"What's the purpose of this?" Evelyn said. "Take us to the train station!"

As we drove away, I looked back at the prison.

Meyer Lacombe opened offices in London and Paris, created a law firm, purchased a luxury hotel, acquired and renovated a castle in Scotland, and brokered many contracts for new construction in Dubai and Qatar through British firms. His attempt at oil in Haiti might have failed, but oil was certainly behind his financial success. Despite all the activity of creating wealth and power, he managed a low profile and kept his name out of the arms trade. This was easier than might be imagined. Meyer wasn't interested in the hardware of arms; he was interested in the technology of arms. His former brother-in-law, Hussein bin Ali, and family members played with guns and bullets, fancied themselves sheiks of the Arabian Desert, coming across the sands on white horses, but Meyer did not. Meyer's fantasy was science, the power of knowledge, and Savensworth Science Laboratory became a portal to his fantasy and a claim to another kind of power.

John Savensworth, the founder of the lab, was a child of Texas oil, but the family business never interested him. Science did. The family fortune was passed on to his two brothers and a cousin, all of whom fancied themselves to be Texas poker players, risk takers. In the beginning there was money enough to fund the laboratory, but within fifteen years, the oil business was sold off, piece by piece, to cover the growing debt and accumulating interest owed to several banks. That left the lab without funds, and his brothers suggested that John close the laboratory. There simply wasn't any money to run it, and John Savensworth wasn't a salesman. He couldn't sell his passion for quantum mechanics for the purpose of fund-raising. He was a different kind of man.

He collected stray dogs because he didn't have the heart to see them on the streets or put to death. He once charged a vet bill to a credit card to have the broken leg on a stray cat attended to while she was nursing kittens. John was once beaten up by members of an inner-city gang in Houston while trying to free a dog that had been chained to a tree on a bare patch of ground. The dog was to be used as training bait for pit bulls. They caught John trying to free the dog and beat him to the ground. As he got to his feet, they tried to put the dog on him, but the dog he had befriended didn't attack, and the gang members then went after the dog. Several days later John managed to retrieve the dog, and she now lived with him at Savensworth Science Laboratory.

It was once suggested that John marry for money. He was an attractive man, with sandy-blond hair, blue eyes, broad shoulders, and a gentle touch. But John couldn't deceive for money. "She'd have to be a scientist," he said to his friend. "Not a patron of the sciences. I couldn't do that."

"Scientists don't have money," his friend said. But John didn't understand this, nor did he grasp the subtlety of human behavior: the meaning behind a glance or the nuance placed on a certain word. John was naïve, his friend later explained to me in London, and this very naivety, his childlike way of seeing things, gave him a fresh way of viewing science. But the meanings behind a woman's touch, the way she might shake your hand, the slight tension around her eye to convey her intentions were lost to him. In front of a woman, he was a child watching a magician appear to remove his thumb with one hand and then make it wiggle while holding it out.

John attended the University of Texas at Austin for two years and then left to pursue his ideas at his own pace, a more accelerated pace than offered at the university. He was basically self-taught in math, physics, and chemistry. He once confessed (to the same friend who provided this background) that one of his greatest pleasures was to think of the nature of calculus. To measure the rate of a certain speed was one thing, but to measure the rate of change of the rate of change was an idea as pleasing as any burst of endorphins. Intellectually he wasn't like the rest of us, his friend said, and for this gift there was a price.

When John Savensworth arrived in London at the invitation of a potential backer, Meyer quietly intervened. He knew John's lab was in financial trouble, and with the completion of Meyer's own analysis of the work being done at the lab, Meyer was determined to have control of any patents that came out of the lab. If the rumors were only half true that John had made significant gains in the design of a quantum computer, Meyer was not to be denied. But under no circumstances would John give up controlling interest in his work, and he leaned heavily toward the original offer of funding from Johnathan Allyson, a member of Parliament. It was then discovered that Allyson was involved in the "cash-for-questions" scandal that included a cabinet minister and several other members of parliament. Meyer was the force behind the affair. He had provided the money and the questions to be asked in Parliament; he then leaked the story to the press, and it was soon learned that the Parliament members had failed to declare their fees for such services. As the story took on a life of its own, it also came to light that Allyson and the minister were paid representatives of a Saudi arms dealer. The scandal destroyed Allyson's reputation and resulted in indictments of perjury against him and the minister.

Intrigue, politics, and international arms dealing left Savensworth very uncomfortable, and he was ready to leave for the States, when Tziporah offered her hand as John was seated in the hotel restaurant, having lunch. This crimson rose in moonlight put John so far out of his depth that he never recovered.

"We have a common interest," she'd said, smiling. "May I sit down?"

This was about the time I returned from Meaux. While I was gone, Adrienne had restocked her supply of pills, and when I came through the door with my bag in hand, she was quite civil. She offered me a glass of wine and didn't ask about the "seminar." After all, why play charades when there's no mystery to the answer. Graham's enthusiasm to see me was real. He had added a few more cars and trucks to his Matchbox collection and several more baseball cards. When I look back on my behavior as a father and a husband, I'm ashamed, but I did what I did and behaved as I did because I am who I am. Why become your own enemy through guilt? We have no more choice over who we are than gravity has a choice in its behavior over matter. The idea of free will is ludicrous.

I learned also that Adrienne was in contact with her parents, both of them. She had written to her father in England and to her mother, who was now living in Tortola in the British Virgin Islands. She was intent on making amends and introducing them to their grandson. Her mother was first on the list.

"My father is easy to be around," she said. "Save him for last—my assuagement. My love for that matter."

"When does this happen?"

"After the fall semester," she said, "we'll visit Mother." There was already a stressed look on her face. "We'll visit Father after you've passed the bar."

When I started the fall semester, I learned that Evelyn Gordon was no longer teaching at Penn. Her contract had been terminated. I didn't know anything of the details, and no one from the faculty would talk about it. I rented a post-office box and wrote to her in Meaux, but I never received an answer. I didn't miss her with a "longing heart"; rather I missed her sensuality as one might miss the summer when it snows or remember an overripe peach, peeled, and held to your mouth to bite into.

We left for Tortola in December, at the beginning of winter recess. Philadelphia was covered with snow, and Adrienne worried the flight might be cancelled. The night before, the wind was treacherous; you could hear it howl against the corners of the house. The snow drifted in large banks, and the snowplows started clearing the road soon after midnight. Adrienne was nervous and agitated each time she pulled the curtains back to see whether our road had been cleared yet. "We *cannot* miss the flight," she said. Her mother never would understand.

Our flight wasn't until noon the next day, but Adrienne was up at 5:00 a.m., calling the taxi service to check and recheck on our reservation and to ask whether they thought the roads were clear enough to travel. This was one of the few times I wished she would take a pill or two, just to calm her, but she was so paranoid her mother might detect something out of the ordinary that she would have suffered anything to convince her she was a "good girl," not the type her mother ridiculed and called trash. Adrienne—the woman who befriended prostitutes, intimidated would-be pimps, and blackmailed weak physicians—was reduced to a child standing in a puddle of her own urine at the threat of a scolding from her mother, while her husband needed twenty years more to see through the fog of selfish youth to understand her pain.

By the time the taxi arrived, the storm had cleared, and the sun was poking through the clouds, and then it cleared completely. The sun was blinding off the new snow. We loaded our bags in the taxicab, and Graham and I got in the backseat. Adrienne held up a finger and said, "Wait a minute." She ran back into the house, and when she returned, I smelled alcohol on her breath.

We boarded the plane without a problem and departed on schedule. During the flight Adrienne drank two or three glasses of wine, and when the plane began its descent into Road Town, she started chewing breath mints.

Beef Island Airport is a sleepy oasis, quaint and traditional, with a "proper" number of private aircraft but nothing showy—a few small jets and turboprops. Adrienne's mother was outside the terminal, near the tarmac, when we departed the plane. She was a thin woman, wiry in appearance, in her late sixties, and had spent too much time in the sun. The skin on her arms and legs had the look of beige leather covered with lotion. But she now took precautions against the sun, she explained—she wore a sunbonnet with a large brim, fashionably inexpensive. "One must blend in, you know." Her mother's name was Edith, but she went by her nickname, "Petter," from English boarding school.

Adrienne wore her public smile—real enough in appearance but forced, her face tightened to hold it in place. Her mother's attention immediately focused on Graham.

"Well, look at you," Petter said. "What a gorgeous little boy!" She took his hand and kissed him on the cheek. Her pleasure over Graham seemed real. She looked at Adrienne. "New dress? Something for gardening?" She turned to me. "You must be Nicholas," she said with an examining look. "Detroit? Must have been an experience..." As she looked away, she added, "At least your fingernails are clean."

She took Graham by the hand. "Let's find the car, shall we?" She gave him "smooches" on the cheek.

I collected our bags, and Adrienne's mother handed me the keys. She and Adrienne got in the backseat with Graham between them. I was the chauffeur. She gave directions to Shellfish Bay and then added, "Careful you don't hit one of those *dark* people. You'll have to pay a fine."

The house was set a hundred yards back from a beach of white sand, and although there was only one floor, there was a stairway up to the front door. There were balconies at each end of the house. The balcony at the west end extended from the bedroom where Adrienne and I slept. A canopy of leafy trees hung over the balcony. At night you could see the lights of Road Town in the distance and above the town a myriad of stars.

I wore cutoff shorts and was often without a shirt, and within a few days, I was brown. Graham's whitish-blond hair turned even whiter, and his blue eyes stood out like the turquoise of the sea. Shellfish Yacht Club was just a short walk away on the beach. There was a bar inside the club and an outside bar. I picked up Graham and set him on the polished mahogany bar inside. The bartender looked askance at this but said nothing. Petter was a member, and he seemed to know who I was. The idea of a life with money and all its privileges was appealing to me, something Meyer Lacombe also saw, early on, and exploited in me.

By early afternoon Petter would announce it was martini time. Her housekeeper was there only three days a week, and today was one of her days off, so Petter prepared and served our drinks. Earlier I had noticed that she had a slight hand tremor, but with her first drink, it soon disappeared. Near the wet bar at the end of the kitchen, she discreetly poured gin into a teacup and, believing she was unseen, quickly drank it and then went about preparing the drinks. When she served our gin and tonics from a tray, I noticed the tension had drained from her face.

The first martini left Petter happy and loquacious as she lavished her attention on Graham, in his bathing suit and copper-toned skin from the sun. She wrapped him in dark-blue and aqua scarves, sheer and flowing, with a long string of pearls around his neck, and even lipstick for accent, to perform on the middle of the carpet. Graham was the center of attention, and he loved it. From all appearances, Petter seemed to be a loving grandmother with gentle patience for children.

By her fourth martini, she had turned her attention to Adrienne. "Where does Graham sleep?" she said to Adrienne, inserting her fork into a piece of fish at the dinner table, never looking up from her plate. "I understand it's a small house." She looked up. "One bedroom?"

"No, Mother. Two."

"Does he sleep in your room? That must be cozy."

There was something going on in the background, concerning sleeping arrangements, of which I was unaware of at the time. But several months later, as Adrienne more freely mixed alcohol with pills, I gleaned hints of a sexual encounter between Adrienne and her father, and her mother knew of it. Adrienne had become, in her mother's eyes, not only trash but also the "other woman."

"No, Mother," Adrienne said, "he doesn't sleep in our room." She didn't look at her mother but at her plate.

"Well, I didn't think so, dear. Not really. Children in a parents' bed? What a thought." She shook her head while never once looking at her daughter. "I can't imagine such a thing." She looked up at Adrienne. "Can you?"

Adrienne pushed her chair back to leave the table. I saw tears on her face.

"Aren't you going to finish dinner?" her mother said, with the pleasure of knowing she had cut deep. "Or maybe you don't feel well. Is that it, dear? Not feeling well?"

Later that night I found Adrienne sitting on the tile floor of the bedroom balcony. The bedroom was dark, but out over the island were the lights of Road Town, and above the village were stars and the depths of space. Adrienne sat with her back against the sliding door and drew on her cigarette in the dark.

"She hates me," she said. "Why did I think it would be any different now?"

I had nothing to offer, nothing to say. I didn't feel particularly accepted by her mother, nor did I feel disliked. Her mother was a stranger to me.

Much later that night, when I awoke to go to the bathroom, I heard noises in the kitchen. Glasses, utensils, ice cubes hitting the floor. I stepped lightly across the carpet. I wore only tight-fitting boxer shorts of thin material. In the moonlight Petter was attempting to drop ice cubes into a tall glass. Her hand shook as she reached for the gin bottle, muttering, "Filthy little bitch…She has the nerve to show up…" She raised the glass of gin to her lips, still muttering, "…just a slut."

We remained for ten days on the island at her mother's house. But most of what might have passed between Adrienne and her mother I didn't witness. I was off in my own world. I spent my time at the tennis club, on the beach, at the yacht club, or fishing for sea urchins from the shallows with Graham, cracking them open and throwing the spongy white flesh back into the water to watch the tropical fish feed on the bits.

The morning we were to leave, I saw Petter on the east balcony in her robe as the sun was rising above the sea. She had a glass in her hand, filled with ice and clear liquid with a slice of lime. "Good riddance…" she said, staring out at the new sun as she lifted the glass to her lips.

At midmorning a taxi arrived at the house.

"Mother isn't feeling well," Adrienne said. "I told her we'd take a cab to the airport."

I carried our bags outside and waited for Adrienne. A moment later she appeared from the house with Graham at her side. She wore large sunglasses as though to hide from the world.

As we waited in the terminal for the airplane to arrive, she said to me, "You'll like my father. You're a lot alike."

"How so?"

"You'll see."

Before I went to prison, John Savensworth and I had dinner together on several occasions. Although he had a keen mind for math and science, human behavior put him out of his element. He had difficulty determining truth from concealment, no matter the body language in front of him. If you told him your favorite color was blue while wearing a bright-red shirt, he would be unaware of the irony. Yet he had the ability to detect a flaw in an idea, no matter how eminent the scientist who presented it.

"Do you realize," he said, "they *invented* a planet to explain Mercury's orbit? They even gave it a name—Vulcan. No one ever had seen this planet; no one had any proof it was there. Yet they persisted with this foolish story." A spot of red wine stained the white tablecloth next to his glass. He scratched at it with his fingernail. "For more than a hundred years," he said, looking up from the spot, "they chased the idea of *phlogiston*. It was supposed to be the secret ingredient that made fire burn. And, again, you couldn't see it, couldn't smell it, couldn't detect it, but everyone said it was there." He shook his head in amusement. "The same is happening now.

Dark matter. I don't gainsay that—dark matter might very well be there; don't get me wrong. But the idea is being treated by some idiots as though it were an unquestionable religion. And let me remind you—you can't see it, can't detect it, and can't measure it. Sound familiar?" He shook his head as he sipped his wine. "As Michelangelo once said, 'When the wine is sour, throw it out.' Why is that so hard to accept? Start over if need be." He shook his head and added, "Why is the need to be right greater than the need for truth?"

Long before this conversation had taken place between John and me, Meyer and Tziporah had entered John's life. They'd arrived with a plan, a purpose. The afternoon Tziporah had seated herself uninvited at John's table in the hotel restaurant, and leaned slightly forward, she revealed a cleavage full of sensual promise. To anyone else the intent of the low neckline, touched by a string of pearls, might have been obvious, but John was without such radar. The subtlety of human behavior was not "science" to him.

Tziporah courted, flattered, ensnared, and trapped him as you might trap a kitten with a ball of yarn for play. She lavished praise on his work, his ideas, and told him how much alike he and her brother were in their love of science. She didn't understand quantum mechanics, she said with a playful laugh; it was too complicated for her. But her brother understood it, and he— her brother, Meyer—thought John's insight into quantum entanglement was just brilliant. Of course, quantum entanglement was all Greek to her, she said, as she caught sight of his watch and the hand-stitched leather band. She reached across the table to take John's hand, to see the watch more closely. She admired his *wonderful* taste, while holding his hand for long moments, until looking up to see the gaze in John's eyes, staring back at her with a view of her cleavage.

Tziporah introduced John to her brother, who was quite eager to meet the renowned scientist. She invited him to dinner at their four-bedroom flat in Park Lane. Oh yes, she explained, she and

Meyer lived together. After all, they were brother and sister. Twins. They had been there for each other since birth.

"How much closer can you get?" she'd said, with a deeper irony than John could have imagined.

"The first time I met Meyer," John said to me one evening at dinner, "I didn't know what to expect. He was quite something to look at. As though I were looking at the Shah of Iran. Persian nobility. Yet he was a Jew. Or he claimed to be. And Tziporah—she wore the Star of David. Nothing gaudy, but it was often pinned to her blouse."

"You ever hear anything out of the ordinary," I asked, "about Tziporah and Meyer? Their relationship?"

"No," he said, a wedge of tomato pierced on his salad fork. "*Oh.*" He suddenly looked up. "That rumor about their closeness? I dismissed it. I mean, who would ever sleep with their sister?"

"What was Meyer's interest in the lab? Back then."

"Quantum computers. The design. He knew a lot about my work." John looked at me as if puzzled. "From the very beginning, he wanted controlling interest…in the lab."

But John wouldn't give up control of the lab. To do so would be to give up control of his thinking, and he needed the freedom to pursue his ideas no matter their direction. He would accept limited funding without attachments, and he would agree to share a percentage of the profits that came from a successful patent, but the patent would remain in his name alone. This was not what Meyer wanted to hear. Meyer wanted control of the technology. He wanted to own it.

When this technology might come to full potential was yet unknown, and this filled Meyer with angst that he might not have his foot in the door at the proper time. A quantum computer, a technology that had the ability to search a multitude of possibilities to a single query, all at the same time, to be (if you will) in "two places at the same time" was in itself a limitless answer. Meyer understood this even better than John Savensworth. As if with tunnel vision, John saw only the science of "solving" the problem. Meyer's genius, however, went immediately to the unknown application. When I first met Meyer, when I first went to work for him, I gradually realized his was the most brilliant mind I'd ever met or possibly ever would. Before this epiphany I had grown cocky and had mistakenly thought I was his equal. I learned otherwise.

⊷⊷ ⊶⊷

Philadelphia was covered with snow for weeks after our return from Tortola. It took me a full day to shovel the walkways, carport, and the entrance to the garage. But I found the strenuous work invigorating, even addictive. I made my way onto the roof and cleared the snow from the gutters and the slate shingles, but I became careless and slipped. I slid off the roof as though I were on ice and landed in a snowdrift below. The next day I was stiff and sore, but it wasn't from the fall. It was from the shoveling, the vigorous activity. This was when I started exercising on a regular basis. Nothing elaborate: fifty push-ups a day and a forty-minute run. The physical and cognitive benefits were enormous. Daily exercise became—and remains to this day—my only deity.

Graham attended private school at this time, with the tuition coming from his grandmother, Petter. The money from South Africa for his education was now funneled into a trust for Graham's later use. Adrienne insisted he would attend the University of Cambridge in the United Kingdom.

I was in my last semester of law school and looking forward to the end. I found the study of law, and its application, no different than the canons of the Vatican. I view man-made law as an atheist views religion.

With the beginning of spring, the crocuses began to appear, first through thin layers of snow and then among the fallen leaves of the previous autumn. The sun was much warmer now, and tiny shoots appeared on the trees. Because it was spring, perhaps, I noticed with even more clarity every woman on campus: the smooth skin of their calves, the movement of their breasts beneath a blouse, a smile in my direction. My thoughts went to Evelyn Gordon, and on a whim, I stopped at the post office to check my mailbox and found a letter from her. It was dated December 3, and this was early April.

There were only a few lines. She said that she had been thinking of our time together in Meaux and that she had decided to take a year away from teaching and that she was planning a trip to London just to hear "English spoken properly." She made no mention that her contract at Penn had been terminated, and I was still curious why it had. I wondered how she was earning a living, what she was doing. Her parents may have been helping financially, or was she living with her husband? I didn't like him; I remembered how he'd referred to me as "your student" and used "Nicky" in place of Nick. His appearance was clean and attractive, but there was something unctuous in his deeper character.

I folded Evelyn's letter and stuck it in a book.

Adrienne didn't want to attend the graduation ceremony at Penn, and neither did I. She said she was too embarrassed to go.

"They'll think I'm your mother." She was still quite youthful looking, but she didn't see it.

In July I took the bar exam, after which we packed to leave for England. Adrienne arranged to have all our mail forwarded to Wilton Crescent, London, to the residence of Lord Nigel Firth.

Over a romantic, candlelit dinner, Tziporah proposed to John Savensworth. She asked him to marry her, straight out and forward. This didn't raise any red flags in John's mind—at least none that he later mentioned to me. Without going into details, he said she was every man's fantasy in bed. Somehow that seemed to be as much thought as he gave it. With a broad smile, Meyer congratulated him on the engagement. "But somehow," John said, "Meyer's heart wasn't in it. He smiled and shook my hand, but something wasn't right." Meyer also mentioned that any funding the lab might need would most certainly be available. After all, they were family now.

Tziporah had insisted they get married in John's native state of Texas, and John was delighted. John had never before given much thought to marriage, let alone the marriage laws of Texas, where all property rights between husband and wife were equal. Meyer had gotten what he wanted.

The honeymoon was short-lived. Tziporah soon returned to London. Meyer had suffered a mild stroke, she said, and as soon as Meyer was feeling better, she would come back to Texas. When John suggested he could accompany her, Tziporah insisted he remain in Texas and continue his work.

"I didn't have a strong mind to go anyway," John later told me in a café over coffee. "Meyer isn't the kind you warm up to." He sipped his coffee and then pushed it aside. It was cold, but he didn't want to hurt the waitress's feeling by complaining about it or simply ask for it to be warmed, so he went without.

Tziporah was eight weeks pregnant when she left for the United Kingdom, but she never mentioned this to John. Once in London, she considered having an abortion, but the servants overheard Meyer oppose such an idea. This was the closest they would ever come to having a child of their own: Meyer's heir.

For nine months, and even a few months after that, Tziporah never told John of the pregnancy or of Pamela's birth. It was as if he were simply too unimportant to consider; after all, would one tell the postman or a waiter the personal details of one's life? When she did come around to telling him that he had a daughter, she did so in a short letter, as one might send a get-well card. When John received the note, it made little impact on him at the moment. He had just gone from creating the outline of a quantum computer to actually having a design supported by math. Hours after having read Tziporah's four-sentence letter, he sat down and stared out the window.

I'm a father!

That evening, without considering the time difference, John called Tziporah in London. A servant answered the phone, and then a moment later, Meyer came on the line. John asked how he was feeling: was there any impairment as a result of the stroke? Meyer hesitated, as if trying to figure out what the hell he was talking about, and then, in a sleepy fog, he realized it was the story Tziporah had told him so she could get away. No, Meyer said, he was feeling fine. But when John then asked about *his* daughter, there was a sudden change in Meyer's tone: it was as if John had said to him, "She's *my* daughter; she's from *my* seed, and don't forget it." This was the beginning of a deep hatred Meyer nurtured against John Savensworth. Although John was no threat to Meyer's importance, or the lasting bond of love and affection Tziporah felt for him, Meyer saw him as a threat. He created it out of an unfounded jealousy, and it was because of this paranoia and his need to control everything that he had ordered me to kill John Savensworth.

I first met Lord Nigel Firth at Heathrow Airport. He was in his early seventies, was very trim, and had the appearance of an athlete. He had white hair—the white of someone who had been blond during his youth—perfectly straight features, and blue eyes. Within moments of seeing him, I liked him. He had an honorable spirit, the kind you might imagine in a knight of old: a man of loyalty without judgment—but of quick and decisive judgment against those he perceived as inane, mean-spirited people prone to "loose judgment." *Leave me alone,* his demeanor conveyed to such people, *but if you must present yourself, be honest about it!*

There was a light in Adrienne's eyes when she looked at her father at the airport. Her smile was warm, and for a long moment, neither said anything as they looked at each other, and then she was in his arms. "I've missed you," she said.

He kissed the top of her head and then held her at arm's length to look at her. Nothing was said, nothing aloud, but a myriad of silent words, whole paragraphs, passed between them at that moment. Adrienne wiped her eyes.

During this scene, tender and secret in its history, a young woman stood next to Adrienne's father. She could have been

Adrienne's double, her twin in age and appearance. Her father introduced her as Carolyn, his wife. I was a little surprised, but from Adrienne's expression, I could see that she wasn't.

"You must be Nicholas," said Lord Firth, offering his hand as the other hand went to my shoulder and then across the smooth of my back in a gesture of acceptance.

"Yes, my lord." The moment was awkward for me. I didn't know how to address him.

"No, please," he said. "Nigel." He turned his attention to his grandson. "Well, young man, how is your tennis game?"

"Good."

"A note of confidence." Nigel laughed. "Excellent, my boy. Excellent."

A Rolls-Royce was delivered to the front terminal, and the attendant loaded our bags in the trunk. Lord Firth drove. Adrienne and Carolyn were cordial enough toward each other, yet I sensed a mild tension between them, if not jealousy.

After a few days, Nigel was more intimate in his conversation with me. He spoke of business dealings and his political views. He was a social conservative, and he was uncomfortable with the idea of "diversity."

"Like attracts like," he said. "It's simple. Birds of a feather… Where do you think *cooperation* comes from? Conflicting cultures? Rubbish!"

But his approach to business was more liberal; he wasn't afraid to invest in a risky stock with the potential of a greater return. This was the first time I'd ever heard the name Meyer Lacombe. In his ever-expanding dealings with the United Arab Emirates, Meyer had acquired an English engineering firm with subsidiaries in the South African mining industry, and this impacted Copperthwaite Mining & Mineral, of which Nigel was a major shareholder.

"This Lacombe fellow—he's behind the cash-for-questions scandal," Nigel said. We'd just finished playing tennis, and we were seated at an outside table, when Adrienne and Carolyn arrived from their match. A waiter from the clubhouse stopped at our table and asked whether we wished to order anything.

"Yes," Nigel said. "Perrier-Jouët. Brut."

"I've got to quit smoking," Adrienne said. "I can't bloody breathe out there." She leaned her tennis racket next to her chair. "So, Father," Adrienne said as she lit a cigarette, "what secrets have you divulged?"

It struck me at that moment, as Adrienne exhaled smoke, that she and her father had each married someone much younger. Was it coincidence?

"Cash-for-questions," her father answered.

"Mother mentioned you were mixed up with Arabs, said you got burned."

"Don't think he's Arab actually. A Jew of some sort. Name of Lacombe, Meyer Lacombe. He's the reason Allyson's been charged with perjury. Terrible business." Her father shifted his weight and looked directly at me. "Allyson was about to help this scientist fellow, when Lacombe stepped in. Actually I was about to help, too. Seemed like a good investment. Allyson assured me this Savensworth was an honest sort. And damn smart."

"So what does he do?" Adrienne asked. "This Savensworth."

"Quantum mechanics," her father said. "Yes, I know, lasers have already been invented. But this chap is ready to take things further. Quantum computers…particles doing magic."

Nigel looked from Adrienne back to me. "Would you be willing to spend some time here?"

"Here?" I asked.

"In England. I can arrange your qualifications. Ellsworth & Ellsworth will sponsor you. I could use help dealing with this Lacombe fellow."

Carolyn spoke up for the first time. "You said this Savensworth thing wasn't worth it."

"No, my dear, not that. Lacombe is interfering with Copperthwaite Mining." He looked at me. "This Arab is a nuisance."

"Thought you said he was a Jew," Carolyn said.

"Really, my dear, what's the difference? Same bloody family."

The waiter arrived with our wine in a bucket of ice. He removed the cork and filled our glasses.

"It's splendid to know you," Nigel said, his hand across the smooth of my back. Then he looked to Adrienne. "Splendid chap…"

Pamela Savensworth had inherited her father's smooth features and sandy-colored hair, while her complexion was darker, a smooth tawny color. Her eyebrows and eyelashes were thick and dark with a natural curl to her lashes. From birth she'd been raised by a nurse and then a nanny. At age five, she was sent to a private boarding school northwest of London. The only emotional bond she knew, aside from the one she had with her nurse, was with her father, whom she visited during the Christmas holidays and summer vacation. She loved her mother but never with the depth or the warmth she'd always felt for her father. Her mother was just there, a memory from infancy, a first impression, a face that became indelible because of its singularity in time, not through purpose. Her father was the warm smile of open arms, a loving hug, a kiss on both cheeks and the forehead.

"He's the teddy bear of my heart," she once said. "With him the world isn't so scary."

Pamela never witnessed her mother and father living together. Tziporah never returned to Texas after Pamela's birth, and John never objected to her absence. Once Tziporah was gone, a forgotten serenity seemed to settle over him again, like an old friend he'd just noticed was missing. Divorce never was discussed. The issues involved were too unsettling for John to consider: property rights and the privileges of fatherhood might come under threat. He also had grown accustomed to the abundant funding for the lab. There was never any need to explain or justify the purchase of new equipment. There was the occasional phone call from Meyer or a visit from a representative of Meyer to ask how things were going—was there any significant progress to report?—or a reminder not to publish anything in a scientific journal without first discussing it with Meyer. Such meddling didn't upset John. The true irritation, John confided, was Meyer's role as surrogate father to Pamela.

Pamela recalled her early years with Uncle Meyer as being fun. While her mother was always a bit stern and distant, Meyer was the Easter Bunny or the tooth fairy come to visit; there was always a present somewhere to be found. Birthdays were true celebrations. Meyer had purchased and refurbished a castle in Scotland on five hundred hectares of land. Pamela's friends from school were invited to a birthday sleepover in the castle. There were clowns, magicians, and presents for all the girls.

"Uncle Meyer made it all happen," she told me one night in a skyscraper lounge in Hong Kong. "But the best part was sneaking off to call Father. I could almost see his smile when he heard my voice."

Meyer saw Pamela as *his* child. He and Tziporah were genetic twins; therefore, Pamela was closer through blood than Savensworth was to Pamela. This was the thinking of Meyer's heart, and he never questioned it. He wanted to be the sole provider of happiness for Pamela. He looked upon her as the Pharaoh's daughter—the daughter he and Tziporah never could have and the sole heir of the Lacombe fortune.

From boarding school on, Pamela was guaranteed a place at Cambridge University. But after only one year, she dropped out. This was a disappointment to Meyer. He had a vision, a fantasy that Pamela would study law and become the head of Lacombe Enterprises of International Law. But the thought of international banking, capital markets, mergers, acquisitions, and dealings with Dubai, Qatar, and the Emirates gave her a headache. In her heart she wanted to be with her father, but then, again, she didn't like Texas. It was too hot and dry. Even the leaves on the trees were covered with dust, she complained.

"You know what Father did?" she said that same night in Hong Kong. "He called Uncle Meyer. And that wasn't easy. They didn't like each other. But Uncle Meyer agreed to move everything—the whole lab—to Maryland. It was wonderful. You could see the ocean from the house. It was almost like being in England."

Tziporah didn't have deep maternal feelings, the instincts of motherhood. She was too much the loner—a rogue vixen. She cared for Meyer, had even killed for him, but as Pamela entered puberty and adolescence, Tziporah had given only passing notice to the changes in her daughter. She saw Pamela as a creature without courage, like her father, lost in a world full of predators. Tziporah didn't have time for such weakness, not in herself and certainly not in others.

"I had a nightmare once," Pamela said, "when I was small. It was terrifying. My father was drowning, and when I tried to save him, I felt *my* lungs fill with water. It was so real."

She looked at me. The lights of Hong Kong and the shimmer of Victoria Harbor were in the background.

"I went running to Mother's room. I woke her, crying. I was afraid. She looked at me; her face was the color of moonlight. 'You silly child!' she said. Uncle Meyer was there too. He sat up, but he didn't say anything. Going back to my room, I was glad—without really thinking about it—that it wasn't my father in there with her."

She sipped her wine.

"It wasn't until much later," Pamela said, "years later, really, that I put the pieces together—about Uncle Meyer and Mother." She set her wineglass down. "But enough about me," she said. "Tell me something about you."

⟞╬ ╬⟝

When I first arrived in England, I thought my stay might last only a few months, but it was many years before I saw the States again. In the fall Graham was enrolled at St. David's Hall. There was a waiting list for admission to St. David's, which extended years into the future, but somehow Nigel made it happen. That same month I received notice that I had passed the Pennsylvania Bar exam, which pleased Nigel. He then arranged for me to take the qualifying tests to practice law in England. Leaving nothing to chance, he produced a copy of each test for me to study beforehand. When I asked how he managed this, he smiled and asked whether I preferred sherry or port.

"Father has a select circle of friends," Adrienne said. "Bloody wide circle actually—and many owe him favors."

One friend was Johnathan Allyson. He and Nigel had known each other for many years, first at prep school and then at university. Nigel was instrumental in organizing Allyson's first campaign for Parliament, and through the years, their mutual alliance in business and politics grew stronger and more complex.

"Cash-for-questions was an ambush," Nigel said. "Allyson was trapped. 'A setup,' as they say in America. And this Lacombe was behind it. Anyone who plays cricket the way this"—he almost stuttered—"Lacombe fellow does, has something to hide. I'm bloody sure."

My task was to find the things that were hidden. At first my motivation was simply to please Nigel, but in time I was drawn to the personality of Meyer Lacombe, the manner in which he ig-nored social rules—cavalier, even romantic in the way he followed his own instincts, his own rules. In the beginning I observed him from a distance, but then I stepped closer and then a little closer still. I imagined I was behind a one-way mirror, and my subject had no idea he was being studied. But when my subject looked intently into the mirror, with his eyes narrowed, I should have known he was now studying *me*.

My first piece of detective work revealed several years of be-havior during the aftermath of the Kennedy assassination. Lee Harvey Oswald had become a household name, and George de Mohrenschildt had been subpoenaed to testify, repeatedly, in front of the Warren Commission. He was asked to explain his as-sociation with Oswald and how the photograph of Oswald and him together had come about. Mohrenschildt never mentioned the photograph of Meyer and Tziporah with Oswald in Haiti. That would have complicated matters even further. He would have been asked to produce the photograph, which would have been impos-sible, since there was only one copy, and I had it.

When I presented my findings to Nigel, he opened the white envelope to remove the photograph and the negative. He held the negative to the light to see the images in reverse. "By George," he said, "this is cracking!" He looked at me. "How on earth did you get this?"

"There was a bit of luck involved."

He looked at the back of the photo. "This name. Who is this? And that number?" He looked at the number again. "A phone number of some kind?"

At this time I was technically employed by Ellsworth & Ellsworth in Central London. The firm was courting a new client in Madrid, and I'd been asked to accompany two other attorneys to assist and observe. Once in Madrid, we attended one meeting after anoth-er, which eventually led up to the Mexican Embassy, where I met

Miguel Camacho, a young man who claimed to be the grandson of the deceased General Maximo Camacho of the Mexican army. Miguel was proud of his family history and kept a scrapbook of newspaper clippings and black-and-white photographs. I love old photographs, so I was quite entertained as he leafed through the pages. Toward the end of the album, I saw a photo that caught my attention, and I asked Miguel whether he knew the story behind it. He said he recently had received a package from his great-aunt in Havana, containing family mementos, and a handwritten letter from Lilia Larine, addressed to the general. The man at the center of this photo was Lee Harvey Oswald, and on one side of him were Meyer Lacombe, Tziporah, and Papa Doc Duvalier.

"Who is this?" I'd asked, pointing to the fifth person, standing on the other side of Oswald.

"That is interesting," Miguel said, looking up from the photo. He went on to explain that his grandfather, General Camacho, had once expelled Mohrenschildt from Mexico. It was matters of the heart, Miguel said. Mohrenschildt had been traveling with a young Mexican woman, Lilia Larine, and General Camacho was jealous of Mohrenschildt. It was believed that the general had had an affair with Larine and that she'd tossed him aside.

"The photo," Miguel said, "was in my grandfather's possession in Havana." He laughed. "Maybe he wish voodoo on him, no? So he keep the photo to—how you say—stick pins in him?"

Perhaps voodoo was the answer, because Mohrenschildt eventually committed suicide, and he wasn't the last person in the photo to do so.

Miguel was called from the room by an adjutant who appeared at the door. Miguel excused himself, and when he left the room, I raised the plastic page cover and removed the photograph. The negative was just behind the print. I slipped them, print and negative, into my breast pocket, but not before noticing a phone number that turned out to be Israeli, as well as a woman's name on the back of the print. When Miguel reappeared, he noticed I had closed the album. He smiled and said, "Shall we join the others for lunch?"

⚔ ⚔

Before returning to London, I sent word to Nigel that I was headed for Israel. The name I'd found on the back of the photograph was Hadassah Hashem. When I called the number, I learned that it was a home for the elderly outside Tel-Aviv. As it turned out, Hadassah knew Meyer and Tziporah in the early years, before they fled to Egypt.

"He wasn't always Meyer Lacombe," she said. "Where he got this name, who knows?" She shrugged. "From thin air maybe."

We were seated outside, beneath a tree. I heard traffic nearby, and although I couldn't see the Mediterranean, I sensed its presence, the faint smell of seaweed and fish.

"You smoke?" she asked. "Cigarettes?"

"No, I don't smoke."

"Good. I don't like the smoking. You get breathing disease."

A nurse in a white uniform brought a tray with tea and some tarts filled with sweet dates. She set the tray on a small table and asked Hadassah whether she wanted a shawl or sweater. Hadassah waved her off. The nurse smiled and turned to leave.

"See this?" Hadassah said of the nurse. "A spy. She think I don't know, but I see. She stop at my room every night. She say, 'You OK, Hadassah?' Every night the same thing. This one I don't trust. 'You OK, Hadassah?' Why say this? I look sick?"

"She seems pleasant enough. Maybe she likes you."

"She is British. You don't hear this? The accent."

"She doesn't sound British."

"The British don't like us. They call us terrorists. When this…" she said, motioning with her head to the surrounding countryside, "under British rule…the Mandate, they call this." She paused. "You don't like the tea?"

56

"Yes," I said and refilled my cup.

I started to fill her cup, but she stopped me. "Just half—stain the teeth."

I looked at her, still holding the teapot.

"Still I have own my teeth." She opened her mouth to show me. "All mine. At my age." She looked over my shoulder toward the building. "The spy. She is watching us."

At this point I lost faith in any information she might reveal concerning Meyer.

"Menachem Yuksek," she said. "That was his name. 'Meyer' he gets from thin air. You don't like the tarts?"

"Oh yes. Thank you."

"You don't touch one. Why?"

I chose a tart and picked up my teacup by the handle.

"Menachem steal guns," she continued, "from British. He sell them to the Irgun. You know what this is, the Irgun?"

"No."

"British call them terrorists. But they were Jews—Jews who fight for Jews. This was the time British rule here. The British Mandate of Palestine. You know of this?"

"Yes," I said.

"The Irgun think the guns Menachem steal from British should be free to Jews. You give them for the cause. But Menachem say no. It is business. You must pay for them. Menachem was shrewd for money." She tapped her temple with her finger. "Smart. But Menachem worked with the Irgun. He fight with them. This is when Menachem flee Palestine—when he change name."

She motioned for me to place my teacup back on the table, and she refilled it from the pot. "You like this tea." She smiled. "Good."

"You are young," Hadassah continued, still holding the teapot by the handle. "Nice to look at. If I was young...but I'm old woman now." She placed the teapot back on the table. "You know how old? Ninety-three. With my own teeth." She paused as if a distant thought had taken her attention. "King David Hotel. You know this?"

"Vaguely," I answered.

"Menachem Yuksek, he supply bombs to blow it up. It is said he do this. I believe is true. This is the time he leave Palestine to Egypt. Meyer Lacombe—he is now this new person. Arab maybe. Who knows?"

She folded her hands in front of her, beneath her ample bosom, and looked at me.

"How did your name get on the back of this photo?" I showed her the photograph. "And this phone number?"

Hadassah looked closely at the photograph. "See"—she pointed to Meyer—"how handsome he is? And she is the reason no woman could have him."

She pointed to Tziporah.

Tziporah didn't care for the world of motherhood. Her heart carried too sharp an edge for anything as delicate as the nurturing of a child. Parenting was left for Meyer to attend to. She didn't feign the part of the obsequious female—she worked alongside Meyer, his equal. Her opinion on any business or political matter was given freely, often with her head resting on a pillow, on crisp sheets, as Meyer lay next to her, listening as though his own thoughts were given voice.

The matter at hand was cash-for-questions and what to do about Johnathan Allyson, whose testimony might well lead to an unforeseen snake pit of trouble. Pamela Savensworth was but a child then, and her mother had warned her never to arrive at her bedroom without first being announced. But the castle was dark, and the night silent—all the servants had gone to bed—and Pamela was afraid, as small children become frightened of the dark. She walked the castle hall toward her mother's bedroom with only moonlight through the stained glass to see by, holding the teddy bear her father had given her.

"I stopped outside their room," she said. "That's when I heard them talking. I heard the name Johnathan Allyson. Years later I asked Father about it—if he'd ever heard of him. I don't know why I asked...The name simply stuck for some reason." Pamela reached for her wineglass. "Look at us," she said, her hand on the stem of the glass, "our reflection in the window. What a handsome couple we are—almost pretty. Actually we are."

"Pamela, I'm old enough to be your father."

"No, you're not. I love the silver through your temples." She traced her fingertips, her painted nails, through my hair. "You're the most distinguished man I've ever seen. Just the sight of you makes me wet..."

"What did your father say about Allyson?"

"Nicky, sometimes you can be so unromantic. Look at this view—the mountains, the night sky, the lights over the harbor... What's it called?"

"Victoria Harbor—and, yes, it's pretty." I refilled my wineglass and waited for her to take the lead again. We were on our second bottle of Dom Pérignon, in the lounge atop the Dragonfly Towers in Hong Kong. This was a period of my life when I drank too much, when my life was out of control.

"I knew Mother would be upset"—she'd picked up at the wrong point in the story—"but I was just a child, and I was frightened."

"What about Allyson? What did your father say?"

"Oh yes." She giggled. "Too much wine. I must be tipsy." She took another drink. "Well, Daddy said..." She suddenly stopped and threw her head back in laughter. "Let me tell you this one thing first. It's wonderful. Then I'll get back to Allyson. I promise."

After another drink—and taking a cold shrimp with her fingers, dipping it in red sauce—she continued. "I said 'Daddy' once in front of Mother. I thought she'd have a cow, I swear. 'Daddy,' she repeated. 'That's slang, something you hear in America. The South. Don't use such language.'" Pamela now had tears of laughter as she continued. "Now this is the best part. I said, 'Well, I'm American and Southern. I'm a *Take'san*.' The accent must have been right on, because she looked at me, her eyes wide. '*You... you...you...*' she stammered. I stared back at her with the sweetest, most innocent grin I could imagine as she continued to stammer, '*You* are English. European!'"

Pamela shook her head in amusement as she finished the champagne in her glass. "That's the only time I ever saw Mother lose her composure. I mean *really* lose it."

The story had impact and meaning for me. For the few years I knew Tziporah close up, I'd never witnessed anything near the loss of composure as Pamela had just described. In my eyes Tziporah was solid, determined, forceful, and calm in the execution of her will, which was, without saying, also the will of Meyer.

"OK, Mr. Impatient..." Pamela sipped her champagne, smiled, and wrinkled her nose in a playful gesture. "Father didn't say much about Allyson—other than he thought his death was suspicious."

"How so?"

"It didn't interest me, so I didn't ask. But he did say he was thinking seriously about selling part of the lab to Copperthwaite Mining. And Allyson was the go-between. Or something like that. Then Allyson was found murdered. Outside some brothel in London—a whorehouse. His throat cut. The tabloids called it the second Jack the Ripper. God, those tabloids are nasty. Yuck!"

The tabloids did try to make it sound quite sorted, but that wasn't Allyson. He wasn't the brothel type. He had a mistress who was much younger than he was. She was a university student at Cambridge, and he paid her rent and expenses, while she studied something to do with art history. If he had lived, I'm sure he would have provided her with an art gallery as well.

"Did he say any more on the subject?" I asked.

"No, but I remember Mother saying—the night I was outside their room—that Allyson had to be dealt with. And Uncle Meyer said, 'I'll have it taken care of.'" Pamela shrugged. "I guess he was going to set his legal people on him. He did that, you know—like his attack dogs or something. But I liked him, Uncle Meyer. Very much. Like a second father."

"Did you hear anything more? Outside their room?"

"No, I was afraid Mother would be cross, so I headed back to my room." She thought for a moment. "But there was something that seemed odd. Or maybe it was just something a child confuses somehow...or has gotten turned around in memory."

"What was that?"

"Mother had a servant...Mohammed something or other. Algenib. He was kind of creepy in a way. Not creepy like a pedophile or anything like that but different. When I look back, I even knew as a child that he was queer—he did to men what I do to you." She crinkled her nose in a playful gesture.

"What about Mohammed?" It was hard to keep her mind off sex.

"Nicky, you're no fun."

I covered her hand with mine. "I'm sorry," I said. I allowed my silence to speak.

"Be nice to me..."

"I will. I promise."

After a feigned moment of pouting, she continued. "Well, I saw Mohammed in the kitchen one day. The head cook was upset with him. She complained that he had taken one of her best carving knives, and he was soaking it in something. It smelled like laundry bleach. He used so much it stunk up the kitchen."

"What was said?"

"Not much. She bitched about him taking her knife, and he ignored her. Went on soaking the knife in that stinking bleach. Matter of fact, he's still around—Mohammed. He still works for Mother."

As I heard this, months—even years—after, certain facts had become clear to me; the pieces fit together as a jigsaw puzzle might shuffle itself in place, magically, without human touch. I wanted to feel less guilty for my actions, to acknowledge my ethereal connection to the circumstances of Tziporah and Meyer Lacombe, but my heart became all the more wretched for the eventual outcome of my deeds.

I signaled the waiter for another bottle of champagne, but Pamela stopped me. "Look what time it is," she said. "Stop before you drink too much."

I looked at her.

"I want you to appreciate what I have in store." She got to her feet. "Now take me to my room."

Time had gotten away from me. I looked again at my watch. Layonna was to meet me in my room in thirty minutes.

"I can't," I said. "I don't feel well. I drank too much."

"You? You can drink gobs more and still do it."

"Not tonight, Pamela. I can't."

"Then just lie there, and I'll do stuff to you."

"I can't. My stomach. I have a headache."

"A headache?" She became upset. "Why do you do this to me?"

My silence made it worse. Pamela turned and walked off in a huff like an angry child.

Adrienne and I were still living in Wilton Crescent with her father and Carolyn when Johnathan Allyson was murdered. Through Allyson, Nigel had taken an interest in Savensworth Lab. Allyson convinced him that it was worth a second look as an investment.

"This Savensworth fellow is pretty sharp," Allyson had explained. "A bit naïve, perhaps, but, nonetheless, he knows his electrons and protons. Inside and out."

Nigel was inclined to invest in the research being conducted by Savensworth—a Texan, he was told, which was interesting, since

Nigel thought Texas fiddled in oil, like those bloody Arabs—but Nigel wasn't all that keen on investing his own money. Not at this point. It was better to have Copperthwaite Mining & Mineral invest and then place himself in position for stock options.

"We can do the same for you," he said with his hand on my shoulder, and his hand then slid across the smooth of my back. "Much safer, you know—no need to look the plonker."

Nigel genuinely liked me. I sensed it, felt it in the way he smiled at me and squeezed my shoulder. It wasn't a father-son thing; it was a man-to-man thing: someone you trust, with whom you share an unrivalled masculinity. A sense of equality, respect. Or was that only wishful thinking?

"Did you know Savensworth is married?" I asked. "To Tziporah. Meyer Lacombe's sister."

"Allyson explained that."

At that point Adrienne and Carolyn came into the library. They wore white tennis skirts along with white jackets that zipped up the front.

"Are we playing tennis or not?" Carolyn said.

Adrienne looked at her father. He winked at her. It brought a pleasant, almost coy smile to her face—a secret I'd glimpsed in the past yet failed to see.

At the tennis court Carolyn and I were paired against Adrienne and her father. Nigel was as athletic as they come. His forehand, his backhand, his charge to the net belied his seventy-plus years. Adrienne was his match, his bookend. I once had played soccer with her—or against her, as we were on opposite teams—and I looked like an idiot trying to block her shots on goal. She was a natural athlete.

As the tennis match continued, Carolyn and I were defeated straightaway—six to one, six to four. It upset Carolyn.

"I'm used to playing with my husband," she said. As we later sipped wine at an outdoor table near the tennis courts, she glared at Adrienne. Adrienne returned her stare as if to say, *Get over it, child.*

"Nigel and I always win," Carolyn continued as her lower lip actually formed a pout. Adrienne couldn't contain her smile as she watched Carolyn whine about losing.

The following evening we learned of Johnathan Allyson's death. We heard the sordid details—or what the tabloids, as well as the BBC, referred to as details—on the news. Allyson's body had been discovered outside an Asian brothel, his throat cut. It was nearly a week later, after toxicology presumably had finished, that it was believed that a common butcher's knife had been the weapon.

"Bovine blood," Nigel said. "That's what the tests indicate. Must have been transferred from the knife."

The tabloids as well as the BBC created the story of the "second Jack the Ripper." You might have thought Scotland Yard would have pursued the truth, but Johnathan Allyson's reputation already had been slandered through cash-for-questions and an indictment for perjury, while his character had been painted in another light. This was the impetus that led me to Paris, to my eventual meeting with Meyer Lacombe.

"Are you sure you want to do this?" Nigel asked me.

"Yes. I'm curious. The stories I've heard. I'm curious to see him up close." This was the cockiness of youth speaking. Today I wouldn't consider, for even a moment, what I was about to do.

"But once you leave the UK," he said, "I can't provide any assistance. You'll live under French law. I'll have no political influence."

But Nigel did provide a reason for me to present myself to Meyer's international law firm. Ellsworth & Ellsworth created a fictitious client for me to represent—a client with connections to Copperthwaite Mining & Mineral, a client wishing to do business in Dubai. In his heart Nigel hoped, I think, that I might return with a piece of damning evidence, something he could use to keep

Lacombe away from Copperthwaite Mining. But after the following afternoon, I was never to see Nigel again. He died while I was in prison.

⊨⊩ ⊩⊨

On the afternoon before my departure for Paris, I returned to the library to speak to Nigel. Carolyn stopped me in the hall.

"I'm sorry," she said.

"Sorry?"

"I behaved so badly the other day. The tennis match."

"Oh, it was nothing," I said and paused a moment so as not to appear rude and then turned toward the library. But I believe her contrition was quite sincere, as she hurried to keep up with me, walking at my side. As we neared the library, I saw that one of the double doors leading into the room was open. I stopped suddenly, and as I did, I grabbed Carolyn by the wrist. It made her turn and face me, her back toward the open door.

"What is it?" she said, startled.

"Oh, nothing. I just…" Past the library door, in the mirror above the fireplace—above the mantel adorned with black-and-white photographs of Adrienne as a young debutante—I saw Adrienne in her father's arms. He held her tightly. The kiss lasted longer than a moment.

"It was silly of me," I said and laughed loud enough to be heard in the library. When I again looked toward the fireplace, there were no images in the mirror.

"Oh…" Carolyn laughed. "For a moment I thought you were going to pull a rabbit out of a hat."

As we entered the library, Nigel was holding some papers from his desk, while Adrienne was across the room, taking a cigarette from a cigarette box. They appeared for a moment as if frozen in time, like actors on a stage, awaiting their cue.

"Oh, Adrienne," Carolyn said, "I'm so glad you're here. I wanted to say I'm sorry for the way I behaved yesterday."

Adrienne appeared relieved. She smiled and said, "It's not worth mentioning. Everything's fine."

Nigel looked up from the papers he held in his hand but wasn't reading. He glanced at Adrienne, and she at him.

The bulk of Meyer's fortune wasn't earned through shipping, his Paris luxury hotel, or the international legal firm Lacombe & Lacombe but in Middle Eastern oil. He received large commissions from Qatar and the United Arab Emirates for having brokered engineering contracts with British, French, and American firms. All such contracts and affiliated works were executed through Lacombe & Lacombe. So it wasn't out of need that he still dabbled in the arms trade. This was more a hobby, a fascination, as a young boy is fascinated for the first time by the sound and power of a firecracker. But Meyer's curiosity went much deeper than sound waves. He was a complicated man with an astute understanding of science and human nature—the behavior of the man across the street or someone whose personality had been reduced to a few paragraphs on paper and who now was about to enter his life. From a position above all the rest of us, he peered across the horizon to a single point in the distance and watched me approach.

Nigel's concern had been that he had thought Meyer wanted to actually own Copperthwaite Mining, when, in fact, Meyer's interest was, and always had been, the ownership of specialized technologies that were the result of the work done at Savensworth Lab. Not until Johnathan Allyson, and then Lord Nigel Firth, expressed an interest in the lab did Meyer take an interest in Copperthwaite Mining. It was simply easier to own the mining company than to deal with these Visigoths, who might screw everything up with primitive moneymaking schemes. Therefore, my pretense, my fictitious client, was based on a false narrative. The only one to see this was Meyer, who, in the pale moonlight of their bedchamber, conveyed the same to Tziporah. What happened next, as it unfolded, was known only to a few.

After my initial introduction at Lacombe & Lacombe, I was introduced to Monsieur Gordon, a close legal attendant of Monsieur Lacombe. I was led into the office of Monsieur Gordon, a spacious room with windows that reached from the floor to the ceiling. Monsieur Gordon was on the phone. He stood in front of the rain-spattered windows with his back to me as he spoke.

"*Oui, j'ai examiné le contrat. Et je suis d'accord.*"

There were a number of framed pictures on his desk, but I couldn't see the images. His conversation came to an end with a few final words, and then pauses, as though he were trying to end it but the person on the end kept throwing in last questions or comments. When he finally turned toward me as he hung up the phone, I was taken by quiet surprise. It was Marcel Gordon, Evelyn's estranged husband. But he wasn't at all surprised to see me.

"Well," he said as he seated himself behind his desk, "you are surprised, no? *Qui*, I see it in the face."

He turned one of the framed pictures around for me to see. The picture was of his two daughters and Evelyn. The girls stood on each side of their mother. All three of them smiled beautifully for the camera.

This was my first notion that something wasn't right. His smile was too satisfied, as though he had trapped a small animal in a cage and would play with it as he wished.

"You have questions, no? Evelyn? She is the good wife again. I should have told you...when you sent your post to her, no? *Qui?* I am so—how you say?—thoughtless, yes?"

Marcel's tone was then businesslike. He explained that he had received the proper background from Ellsworth & Ellsworth and that a contract for raw materials from Copperthwaite Mining to a subsidiary of BAE systems was favorable to all involved. This had the sound of new information to me, and I thought it best for me to say little on the subject until I had talked to someone at Ellsworth.

"We wish to provide for your comfort," he said.

He then led me to an office that had been set aside and equipped for my use. There was also an assistant, a secretary whose English, he assured me, was passable.

"Tomorrow you will meet Monsieur Lacombe." He turned to leave and then stopped and again faced me. "Monsieur Lacombe—he is eager to meet someone so interested in his life."

In my yet-unknown future, Pamela Savensworth would one day sit across from me with the innocence of a child. Her features were soft, without straight lines or sharpness, but smooth with youth; her eyes were so brown you could barely see her pupils.

We were on a private yacht anchored off the shores of Macau the night she related yet another side of Tziporah, a behavior that didn't surprise me. The yacht belonged to Sheik Mohammed bin Rashid Al Zayed. The sheik didn't have a strong mind for business, but his family connections were useful to Meyer, so Meyer indulged the sheik's fantasy that he, the sheik, was excellent at blackjack. The sheik enjoyed having people surround his table to watch him play. It's my feeling that these spectators were there to watch the never-ending train wreck that would unfold from the sheik's hand. He might sit there with eighteen showing, peek at his third card, and then ask for another card. He might bet a million pounds sterling on such a hand.

"You think he actually believed he could win?" Pamela asked as she told a similar story. "I mean, he doesn't really look dumb." She shrugged as she reached for her wineglass. "Uncle Meyer was always nice to him, though. But what did that prove? He was even nice to his enemies. You never knew…"

We were on the main deck, just the two of us for dinner. The night skyline of Macau was reflected in the harbor. Our table candles flickered lightly in the breeze, and then the breeze calmed and faded to nothing. The candles reflected in Pamela's eyes, the way I'd once seen candlelight reflect in Tziporah's eyes. Pamela, in discreet moments, was the mirror of her mother.

"Don't you ever eat meat?" she asked.

"Sometimes…but finish your story."

"I get off on rabbit trails. That's Daddy's favorite expression… 'rabbit trails.' You'd think science was one big rabbit patch."

Over Pamela's shoulder, I noticed the sheik was watching us from the bow of the yacht. He was in his late fifties, with dyed hair, a dyed beard, and dyed eyebrows. He had several wives, and from the way he looked at Pamela, I knew he wished to add her to his collection, but he feared the wrath of Tziporah. Against another man he would have drawn his mythical Arabian sword to slay his rival and drag Pamela off to his harem, but the thought of facing Tziporah brought common sense to this fool.

"Anyway," Pamela continued, "Uncle Meyer was always having work done on the castle…Sounds odd, doesn't it? 'Work done on the castle.' Daddy said Uncle Meyer lived in a fantasy world. They just didn't like each other."

It was hard to keep her on track, so after I nodded, I asked again, "So how does your mother come into it? The story you started?"

"Yes…They were working on a room next to that giant kitchen—the workers were, that is—but this was the weekend, so they weren't there. Anyway, Uncle Meyer heard a noise. It came from a hole in the floor, next to the wall. Not a steady noise but a here-and-there noise. Like something was moving around in there. He looked in the hole, but he didn't see anything. He got to his feet and went off to get a tool or a stick—or something…I don't know.

"That's when Mother got down on her knees and looked in the hole. But she couldn't see anything, either. Now you won't believe what she did then—she stuck her hand down there. In the hole!' She searched around and then let out a short cry, 'You bastard!' But she kept reaching around in there, trying to grab…whatever. After she cursed again and again, with the squealing in the hole still going on, she lifted out a rat. She slammed the rat against the stone floor, hard, and then tossed it to the wall. I couldn't believe it. Her hand was all bloody. That rat must have bitten her like a million times, but she wouldn't give up. She kept going after it—bloody hand and all."

Pamela reached for the champagne bottle in the ice bucket and removed it by the neck. Not until the weight of the unbalanced bottle pulled at her wrist down did she come back from her thoughts. "Oops, I almost spilled it…"

I reached for the bottle and refilled her glass.

"Sometimes I think she's nuts. And then—you won't believe this—Uncle Meyer arrived with a towel and bottle of rubbing alcohol to clean her wounds. It was like he knew—before he'd even left—that she would do that. Anyway, the doctor came from the village and stitched her up and gave her shots, I guess…so she didn't get, like, the plague or something."

Pamela thought for a moment and then looked at me. "When you think about it…it's kind of spooky…the way she wouldn't let go of that damn rat. She wouldn't stop."

I looked across the bay, over my shoulder, toward Hong Kong. Was my fate that of the rat?

I had spent a little more than a year collecting information for Nigel Firth. This included several interviews with people who claimed to have known Lacombe in the past. For the most part, their stories held together when compared against one another. There were petty grievances (I should have been invited to such-and-such dinner party—"It was bloody rude of him"—and so on), but Meyer was basically described as a man of calm certitude, calculating in business, and, on the surface, polite in personal matters yet unforgiving in the face of even an imagined insult.

Up to this point, I had yet to actually meet anyone in Meyer's personal life. That followed our first meeting.

The young woman who was to be my secretary stepped into my office hours before I was to meet with Meyer. She came toward my desk—my empty desk; I had nothing to do and no idea why I'd been given a desk in the first place—with several pages from a large printout.

"Monsieur Gordon *a demandé votre présence cette après-midi.*"

"I'm sorry, but I don't speak French."

At that point Marcel Gordon came through the open door to my office. His smile wasn't exactly a smirk but a look you might feign to a naïve child.

"The printout," he said. "Ah, yes—numbers for your client. You wish to see them, no?"

I was being asked questions about matters that hadn't been discussed. My discomfort grew. "And the young lady here…you said she spoke English?"

"Well…" He smiled. "She is—how you say?—learning."

I looked at the printout. It was in French.

It was early afternoon, two o'clock, when I was told Monsieur Lacombe wished to see me. Meyer didn't keep an office at Lacombe & Lacombe. I was taken to Hôtel Ritz.

Through the revolving doors, the hotel lobby could have been the palace of Louis XVI. Just inside the entry, a young woman in blue livery nodded in a polite yet subtle manner. At the center of the lobby, there was a circular table adorned with purple, lavender, and yellow flowers, while above the table hung a crystal-white chandelier. To the left was a grand stairway carpeted in red-and-gold floral with a navy trim; the carpet gave softly beneath my step. At the top of the stairs, on the mezzanine level, was the office of Meyer Lacombe.

As I ascended the stairs, a woman in a red skirt, white satin blouse, and heels was waiting for me at the top.

"Monsieur…" She held her hand toward the door. She pressed a discreetly placed button next to the door to announce her entrance with a guest.

Meyer stood behind his desk, his back to me, facing tall windows, with the Eiffel Tower in the distance. The horizon stretched across the city in a wispy vapor with the pink glow of the sun through the gauze of afternoon light.

"Pretty, isn't it?" Meyer said, still with his back to me. "But I prefer London…or Scotland. They're more serious in nature. In Paris there's frivolity." He turned. "Please, Nicholas…sit down."

He wasn't as tall as I'd expected—perhaps my height, less than five eight. His dark hair and eyes were striking: his hair wavy, full, and streaked with silver; his eyes didn't appear as though they were given to smiling. He took a seat behind his desk and opened a folder. There was a simple gold band on his ring finger and nothing else, not even a watch.

He opened a pair of glasses—readers—slipped them on, glanced up at me as if to take in my full appearance, and then returned to the folder. He removed a black-and-white photograph, studied it for a moment, and then placed it on the desk, next to the folder. He removed another page.

"Very impressive score." He read from the report of the test I had taken at Motorola. He had the original. "Your ability to see relationships...where others see nothing..." He nodded, still looking at the page, as though in approval or perhaps disapproval.

He turned to the next page, pausing to read. "Your transcripts," he said, "I'd say the less-than-perfect grades were from boredom."

It wasn't a question.

"I see here," he continued, "when you were challenged, your grades improved." He read for a moment longer. "Do you find it difficult, Nicholas, dealing with the less gifted?" He didn't look at me when he asked this.

I grew more uncomfortable.

He removed his glasses to look at me. "Law school must have bored you." He replaced his glasses and then went back to the folder. "Did you know when you met your wife"—he looked to the previous page and then back again to the next page, as if to recheck what he'd just read—"in Detroit...in a bar, I see...she was of patrician class?" He waited for me to answer and then said, "That *was* a question."

My palms were sweaty. "No...I didn't know."

"I believe you." He looked back to the page. "Do you like your father-in-law, Lord Nigel Firth?"

I felt as though I were ten years old again and being questioned by my father—with the same fear in my heart.

"Yes," I said.

"What does he know about you? Your father-in-law."

I had no answer.

"Does he know your grandfather was a Hungarian Jew?"

"No."

"Does your wife know?"

I shook my head. "No."

"So, Nicholas, you're a social climber, aren't you?"

Those words, such a description, "social climber," never had come to my mind before, and since it was such a foreign thought, I now had the courage to deny any such description.

"No," I said. "I wouldn't say that."

"But you worked in a factory. You never finished high school. Your father was a carpenter. He carried on an affair with his neighbor...a scandalous affair, from all accounts." He held a picture of my father in his hand. "Handsome man," he said. "Blue-eyed Jew." He placed the picture back in the folder. "Do you think of yourself as a Jew?"

"No."

"Of course not. Look at you. You look as though you're from Norway, Sweden...Iceland. Do you believe in God?"

For a moment I said nothing. I didn't see the connection.

"If you were given a choice," he said, holding his reading glasses, "God or truth, which would you choose?"

Without hesitation I answered, "Truth."

He closed the folder and looked at me. "Would you like to work for me?"

I had no answer. I was surprised, perhaps startled, confused. Yet in another part of my mind, my soul, I was deeply flattered.

"You'll work with my legal team."

"I've never actually practiced law."

"You have information," he said. "Information you've collected through the years, through education, from things you've observed, read, and heard. You have the ability to create new information from what you've collected. That's a rare talent."

It was at this moment I felt the need for him to like me. Not out of any need to further my usefulness to Nigel Firth, or to please Nigel, but to be looked upon with sincere favor by Meyer Lacombe.

The man's heart was seductive, and I had yet to learn how dangerous he was.

⚊⚊

My first meeting with John Savensworth happened before I went to prison. Meyer had arranged the meeting, the purpose of which, according to Meyer, was for me to know something of Savensworth and his work. To what end Meyer never disclosed. That came together later. The meeting with John Savensworth was to be a blacktie dinner, and it seems Meyer knew beforehand that I didn't have evening clothes. He sent his tailor to my "office" to measure me for a tuxedo.

The tailor was an elderly man, Peterus, who disclosed that he was a Hungarian Jew. There was something warm and grandfatherly about him. His eyes were greenish-gray and his hair a dull gray. His teeth were a faded yellow from pipe smoking that he said he'd once tried to give up. "That didn't last," he said with a flick of his hand, as if to dismiss any future effort. His clothes were baggy and in need of pressing.

"Mr. Lacombe doesn't often share my services," he said while measuring across my back, my left arm extended. "You must be special, young man." His breath smelled of apples and tobacco.

I asked questions about Lacombe, but Peterus didn't answer. He continued to take measurements. At the end of our session, as

78

he put his tape measure and notepad in his coat pocket, he said, "Mr. Lacombe rescued me."

"Rescued?"

"I was in Turkey. Istanbul. Jews aren't treated well there. Tolerated maybe…He brought me to London and then to Paris." He nodded as though agreeing with some distant memory.

"Is Mr. Lacombe a Jew?" I asked.

He smiled. "Of course. You think a Muslim would help a Jew? A Muslim," he said, shaking his head. "A Muslim would rather roast and eat me." He chuckled. "And, of course, spit me out!"

There was something charming and endearing about this old man, Peterus, this Hungarian Jew, and in the privacy of my heart, I imagined my grandfather had been the same kind.

Several days before my meeting with John Savensworth, Marcel Gordon informed me, "Your things have moved."

"My things? Moved?"

"How you say…?" He motioned with his fingers as though they were entwining string. "Your belongings, *oui?*"

"My belongings. Where?"

"L'Hôtel on Rue des Beaux Arts. Your new address. You are also to…" He thought for a moment. "*Dîner à l'hôtel avec* Monsieur Savensworth *et* Madame Savensworth. Monsieur Lacombe…he made this for you."

Meyer had arranged the new accommodations in order to keep a better eye on me and to seduce me even further into the world of luxury. When I arrived at my new address, there was a bottle of cold champagne and hors d'oeuvres in my suite. The bedroom was decorated in a rich fabric of red, crimson, and gold. The window drapes were pale olive. My clothes had been pressed and hung in the closet, and a note on the dresser informed me that a few items had been sent to the cleaner's. I slipped off my shoes and poured a glass of champagne. The carpeting cushioned each step. I sat down on a velvety red chair and ran my hand along the arm; somewhere in the fabric, there was silk. I looked around. *How far is this*, I asked in satisfied thought, *from the factories of Detroit?*

Three days after I had met Peterus, he arrived at my suite with the tuxedo. I had imagined more fittings, alterations, and further measurements with white chalk, but there was none of this. The fit was perfect, as though the fabric contained my DNA, my most secret dreams.

I looked into the mirror. A smile came to my face as I gazed at the person I wished to be and who now was before me.

"Peterus, I can't thank you enough." I looked sideways in the mirror and then turned again. "It's beautiful. Nothing has ever fit me like this." I stepped back, staring at my image in the mirror. "I'm speechless."

He removed a pipe from his suit pocket and placed it between his teeth. He stepped sideways to have a better view of his work as he nodded to himself. He smiled, his thumb and index finger inserted in his vest pocket.

⊷⊶

My meeting with John Savensworth took place in the hotel dining room the following evening. The dining room was formal, baroque in appearance, yet intimate. Heavy drapery covered the windows, parted here and there, and seemed, at various points, to descend from the ceiling. The seating was upholstered in blue elegance, plush; the tables were covered in white linen; and the lighting was as soft as candlelight, yet better, more flattering.

Savensworth was in black tie, seated at a table, alone. He seemed to be examining the hors d'oeuvres. He had cut one in half with a table knife and was inspecting the tiny parts, spreading them apart with the end of the knife. I was escorted to his table.

He looked up. "Nicholas?"

"Yes," I said. He stood—he was well over six feet tall.

"And you are John Savensworth." I offered my hand.

"Please sit down."

He had sandy-blond hair, thinning and pushed to the side without thought or care. His smile was warm, his eyes brown, crinkled at the corners, sincere, without tension or pretense. He was comfortable with himself—as if he had never given thought as to how he might appear to others. I was at ease in his company.

"Copperthwaite Mining & Mineral, correct?" he said.

"Yes. Well, not me—my father-in-law—the family, that is the Firths."

"I've received an offer of funding from them."

"Is that what brings you to Paris?"

"No." He laughed. "Not this time anyway. It's my daughter, Pamela. It's her eighteenth birthday."

A young man in a white shirt, white bow tie, and red vest appeared at my side. He asked if I wanted anything to drink. I glanced at John. There was a drink the color of bourbon with ice next to his plate. "No, I'm fine," he said.

I ordered wine and asked the young man to decide for me.

"A coming-out party?" I asked and then realized I might have used the wrong word, the wrong phrase. "A young debutante."

"That's what her uncle calls her. A debutante. To *me* it's her birthday, and I love her to pieces. So I'm here."

"Is the ball here in Paris?"

"No, London. And then off to Scotland…Meyer's castle." He smiled, his eyes crinkling at the corners, the same look I would one day see in Pamela. "A little pretentious, don't you think? A castle? But he's her uncle, and she loves him. So I say nothing." He took a sip from his drink. "And there's her mother, Tziporah…" There was the sound of resignation to his voice.

The young man in the red vest arrived back at our table. He opened the wine, poured a sample, waited for my approval, and then filled my glass.

"You'll be at the ball, won't you?" I said.

"Oh yes. Yes, indeed. But not the castle." He placed special emphasis on "castle," as if it were a point of amusement. "I'll return to Maryland. My work at the lab. And you? Are you going?"

"No," I said. "I'm not family."

Days later, after the ball, I checked the newspapers to see pictures of the young debutante. At eighteen, she had her mother's eyes and mouth but her father's coloring. She was very pretty but with a slight arrogance to her smile, the look of a child who'd never been told no, at least not in a serious way.

Thirty minutes went by in conversation that was neither idle nor in any manner trivial. He was a serious man, but in no way did he take himself seriously—his work he definitely did, but he didn't confuse himself with his work.

Meyer and Tziporah still hadn't arrived. They were more than thirty-five minutes late. John said he'd never known Meyer to be late; Tziporah maybe but not Meyer. It was then that I noticed Tziporah being escorted to our table. But her escort wasn't Meyer. Her escort wore a dark-gray suit with a faint stripe to it and a pink necktie. His hair was dyed, as were his beard and eyebrows—dyed almost black.

John and I stood.

"I'm sorry," Tziporah said, "but Meyer can't make it. He sends his apology. And I'm sorry to say I can't, either. I've promised to attend to something for Meyer."

Before she left she introduced her escort. "John, Nicholas, this is Sheik Mohammed bin Rashid Al Zayed." The words rolled from her mouth without effort or thought, as though Arabic were a nursery language.

After our brief introductions, she said, "Now I must be going." As she turned to leave, she stopped. "I'm sure you two will get along…"—she paused and then continued—"…just fine."

We sat for a moment or two in silence. John finished his drink. "Maybe I'll have another," he said. He looked at me. "I know what you're thinking. Why did I marry her?"

I waited in silence.

"I was young," he said. "Young. And I thought she saw romance in my work. But it was Meyer who saw the romance. He was captured by the technology—the possibilities—and he wanted to own it. And she gave it to him. They bestow presents upon each other, and I was one of the presents…or my lab was." He looked at me. "Yes, I know about them. Not at first, but now I know."

My heart went out to him. Not for the loss of Tziporah but having been duped, so openly made a fool, and for the possible loss of his work and his daughter.

"Divorce isn't possible," he said. "I would lose my lab and most certainly my daughter."

Our waiter was nowhere in sight. I looked for him a second time and then reached for the bottle of wine. I poured some into John's empty glass, still with ice cubes, and then refilled my glass.

"Thank you," he said.

He picked up his knife and pushed the dissected hors d'oeuvres around on his plate. "Do you know what this is?" he asked.

"I have no idea."

The work I was given had nothing to do with Copperthwaite Mining & Mineral or my fictitious client. It had nothing to do with anything I'd ever seen before. There were ledgers and spreadsheets and legal documents, half of which were in French. When I asked my young secretary, Pauline, about this, she smiled sweetly.

"*Cher monsieur, pour votre signature, s'il vous plaît.*"

"Pauline, I know you can speak English. I've heard you. Please."

"*Mais*...I will make the mistake...and this is...dumb, no?"

Her smile and her innocent manner, her unaffected need to please were too sincere to feign. I signed what she put in front of me.

I received several invitations to lunch with Marcel, but I refused, always having excuses—a dentist appointment; a meeting with my banker, the butcher, the candlestick maker, the tent maker, whatever—all of which he certainly knew were false. If he'd had respect enough to *show* his dislike of me, even behind a smile, I might have lunched with him, if only to learn something of Evelyn's "new" life.

I did lunch with Pauline, though. The first time I asked her, she looked at me. "*Moi?*" She pointed to herself as if to be sure I wasn't talking to someone else.

The seasons changed early that year. I had found a little café off a side street where the sidewalks were checkered with brown leaves and sunlight. There were only five tables in the café, and the chef-owner-waitress was always "stepping out for a moment." She'd hold up a finger to indicate she'd return shortly, while wiping her hands on her white apron as she hurried out the door. I glimpsed her a few times on the sidewalk talking to a young man. He appeared much younger than her, but it seemed he was her boyfriend, her lover. A quick kiss and she'd return to the café apologizing. "*Désolé, désolé...*"

Pauline and I shared an open-face sandwich of cheese, tomato, and olives, toasted under the broiler. Pauline bit into her half of the sandwich, and a long string of cheese pulled away and fell over her chin. Her eyes looked up at me, and she blushed. "*Désolé.*"

"Why are so many documents in French?" I asked. "The ones I am to sign."

She shrugged. "It is the way Monsieur Gordon say to do."

"What are all those spreadsheets for? The ledgers?"

"It is for the money, no? To know where it go."

"Shouldn't there be a copy in English...if I'm to oversee it?"

"Monsieur Gordon say no." Here smile was innocent and sweet. She simply did as she was told and thought nothing of it.

The young man from the sidewalk tapped on the café window. Our waitress-owner looked up from the kitchen and blew him a kiss.

The afternoon that Marcel Gordon came into my office and asked me in a jovial manner to sign a certain document, I should have known something was wrong. Very wrong. I hadn't seen or heard from Meyer in many weeks, and when I asked about this, I was told he was still in Scotland. John Savensworth had returned to Maryland, and Tziporah was supposedly in the Middle East. When I asked if that meant she was in Israel, I received no answer. There were also a number of businessmen from the United Arab Emirates visiting the offices of Lacombe & Lacombe. Various meetings were held in one office and then another—some hurried and some not—all with an air of secrecy. When I asked Pauline about this, she gave me her innocent smile and said she hadn't noticed and went about whatever she was doing.

The document Marcel Gordon had asked me to sign, which I did, had the appearance of a legal brief, but, again, it was in French. It was stupid for me to sign it; I know that. But it doesn't change the outcome. As it turned out, it was a signed confession, a plea bargain, if you will. I unknowingly had admitted to embezzling millions of dollars from accounts in the United Arab Emirates. The French authorities arrested me that same day.

⊷⊶ ⊷⊶

My "trial" started in late fall. I saw the first traces of snow through my solitary window high above the Paris streets. Even though it was dark, I saw the snowfall lightly past the window opening. And then the nights turned clear and cold and starry dark. There was no heat in my cell. I often ran in place and did push-ups to keep warm. Sometimes I awoke in the middle of the night and lay in my bunk and stared up at the ceiling.

Months earlier I had pleaded not guilty. At first I was outraged. The whole thing was preposterous. There was no proof—how could there be? I'd never done such a thing, never even considered it, never fantasized about such a thing. My outrage then turned to humor. This was a mistake, a ruse, a way to test me under pressure, all the while knowing full well, deep in my heart, the truth that faced me. But my outrage, my protests, and my attempts to reason with the authorities were met with silence as they stared at me with blank faces.

During the "trial" I was given headphones to hear translated proceedings. My attorney often gave long sighs and glanced at his watch. Everyone was bored but me. My attorney advised me that my sentence could be as much as eighteen years. Hopefully, he indicated, I would serve it in France, not Dubai.

The case against me was put forth: I had created false documents, the prosecution claimed; I had opened an account in Quebec, Canada, to accept transfers from Paris and Dubai. The paper trail was set out in detail, along with my signatures on all required documents. Nine million dollars now sat in an account under my name in a Canadian bank. I argued that the "confession" was in French, and I'd had no idea what I was signing. This was met with silent pity or amusement. At this point I realized the hopelessness of my argument, and I was resigned to any outcome.

While waiting for judgment and the pronouncement of my sentence, I heard from Adrienne. The letter had been opened, examined by the censors, and passed on to me in a crumpled state.

Mother has arrived from Tortola. She's quite ill. Cancer. She's living in London, but I'm afraid she won't be with us long. She still smokes even though she coughs blood into her hand. And someone (the nurse, I think) is sneaking gin to her. She'll never change. And she still hates me. (Father is devastatingly sorry he let you go to Paris.)

I will not divorce you. You're like my firstborn.

The court soon delivered its judgment. Guilty. A few days later, I was sentenced to fifteen years in a French prison. I was taken to La Santé Prison in Paris.

The first year was difficult. Hard to endure. Very hard. The strangeness, isolation, the unknown, and the brutality of the guards. My head was shaved and left bleeding from the dull clippers. I was then given a jumpsuit to wear. It had been washed many times, but it still smelled of onions, urine, and the faint odor of vomit. When I first put it on, I raised my arm to smell the sleeve. I suddenly saw stars and couldn't get my breath, as I found myself doubled over on the floor. A guard kicked me in the ribs and told me to get up. It was made clear through words I didn't understand that I wasn't to smell the clothes unless I was told to. After several months, I no longer could smell the vomit.

Every hall I was led down, every turn and every room I entered held the fear of sexual hyenas waiting to grab me by the throat. This happened once, and I bit the arm that grabbed me until it bled, gnawing harder and harder to the bloody bone. A guard appeared and dragged the attacker off me. I was then kicked, beaten, and thrown against the wall by the guard. My head hit the concrete and opened a cut just above the eyebrow, the left one. I'd gotten off lucky. In my cell I rinsed the cut with water and held it together, pinched between my thumb and forefinger, until the bleeding stopped. I sat that way for hours, on my bunk in the dark.

Fortunately I didn't have a cellmate. I lived by myself in a six-by-eight cell with a stainless-steel commode. I was given water in a plastic bottle, one quart a day. You were given one toothbrush every year. If you broke it, lost it, ruined it, or it was stolen, you didn't get another until the following year. Your mouth could rot. It was then, lying one night in the dark, feeling my teeth with my tongue, when I realized I was in *my own care*. There was only me. It was like that day in traffic court in Philadelphia when I realized that laws aren't created for me, for my good, or for the "public good." Rather they're the will of someone else, imposed on you for their benefit. For the first time in almost two years, a smile came to my face as I lay in the dark, staring up at my open window, with the faint smell of spring coming to season. At that moment I knew I was smarter than anyone who held me there, and I would slowly find a way to escape…patiently.

Months later I received another letter from Adrienne, crumpled and torn at one end. With the letter there was a book, a paperback, *See It & Say It in French,* and a French dictionary. Outside my window I heard the sudden downpour of a summer rainstorm and smelled the ozone. I unfolded the crumpled letter.

Mother has been dead two years now. That's easy to live with, her death—it's even a blessing; I no longer feel her judgment. Her hatred.

But now Father is gone. It happened so suddenly. He went to bed feeling fine, but he never woke up. His doctor is puzzled. Everyone is. Just that day we'd played tennis together. He was so fast, alert. No one has an answer. I miss him so much!

He left everything to me, his entire estate, and just a pittance to Carolyn. She's furious; she smashed things, threw glasses against the wall—threw framed pictures of me. The next day she said she was sorry, but it meant nothing to me. A well-rehearsed play. I don't get it. I don't. What did she expect? She was just my surrogate.

p.s. I'm leaving for South Africa tomorrow. Grandmother is ill. Graham is going, too.

Think kindly of me.

I knew I would see Adrienne again. When? I had no guess. But I would see her again.

Thinking—planning—happens even when you aren't conscious of it. Ensconced in your mind is an idea without form, only purpose. Around that purpose, unconscious thought crackles like electricity, and it never stops. In your dreams and just outside peripheral view, it never stops, because it has the importance of life itself. Something that had happened days or months ago might pop into my thoughts, and within that memory might lay the blueprint to my escape. It might be an incident menial to another person—and at the moment it happened, even menial to me—but then the obviousness of it would reveal the silence of genius. A thing overlooked because it was so obvious. This was what I waited for, patiently. The glimpse of an incident or a word said one too many times, unknowingly, by a guard, which said, *Here is your blueprint, your opportunity—follow carefully an unconscious mistake of the guards; it will lead to your opening, your chance at freedom.*

For five years I collected images, words, routines, seemingly unrelated events to form a single plan of escape, when the unexpected happened. I should have known something was different. For three or four months in a row, the brutal prison barbers hadn't shaved my head. My hair was allowed to grow. Then a single guard appeared one morning at my cell. He opened the door and motioned with his finger for me to follow him.

I was taken to a shower area, one I'd never seen before. There was both hot and cold water—and soap. The lather was thick and smelled of green leaves. For a moment I stared at the foamy bubbles in my hands and running down my legs. With dark humor I wondered whether it was my last shower, as one is given a last meal.

I was then given denim jeans, leather shoes, a white shirt, and a corduroy sport coat. The guards who managed this were new to me. They were older and less sadistic. I was led to the prison exit, which opened onto a street lined with the trees of autumn. The guard who accompanied me was much older than me. He gave a faint smile and offered his hand. Stunned at what was happening, I shook it.

The prison gate opened, and I stepped through to the other side.

In the street in front of me was a chauffeur-driven car with the engine running, a silver Rolls-Royce. The windows were slightly tinted, and a woman sat in the backseat. The chauffeur had gotten out and motioned with his hand toward the rear door, but he didn't open it for me. As I approached the door, I saw my reflection in the window. It stopped me, my hand reaching for the door handle. For an instant I thought it was someone else, someone behind me. I looked so much older. My temples were streaked with silver, and there were lines at the corners of my eyes. The young man of near-feminine beauty was gone. An instant later my hand took hold of the door handle, while my eyes remained fixed on my image. I pressed the latch, and as I pulled the door open, I continued to stare at my image, which now shifted with the angle of the window. I was pleased with this man who now opened the door for me. It was the pleasure of maturity, no matter how ephemeral, the moment of a newly held confidence.

Tziporah watched this unfold. Whether she knew anything of my thoughts at this moment was unimportant to the future.

"Hello, Nicholas," she said this as if she believed *she* held the advantage, but there was no surprise in my voice.

"Tziporah, how are you? *Bien, j'espère.*"

"My—we've acquired a new language, I see. But I guess you had time to kill. Is that right, Nicholas? Did you have time on your hands?"

I sat comfortably on the plush seat, the width of the car between us. "That's a lovely perfume you're wearing," I said, looking at her and then toward the driver and then out my side window. "It's such a pretty time of year, isn't it? Some might think the colors are garish, but I don't." I looked back at her. "What do you think? Garish?"

There was a slight tension around her eyes, as if she were holding back anger that I hadn't acknowledged relief or gratitude at having been released from prison. *The weather,* her eyes seemed to say. *That's what he's going to talk about? Weather!*

"Meyer wishes to see you," she said. "I'm sure you'll make the right decisions…seeing that you've had so much time to think." There was finality to her tone—the same tone I'd heard Adrienne's mother use toward Adrienne—as if to say, *I know, and you know I know.*

I was taken to L'Hôtel on Rue des Beaux Arts.

"You'll meet Meyer tomorrow," she said. "For lunch."

I didn't ask where or what time. I got out of the car without looking back and walked toward the hotel entrance. Reflected in the glass doors of the hotel, I watched the car pull away from the curb. This wasn't arrogance, exposing my back in such a way, ignoring Tziporah, but a new sense of awareness, as a lion tamer might reenter the cage after having once been mauled. The element of surprise was gone.

I was in a different suite on a different floor, but the apartment and furnishings looked the same. Almost nothing had changed. My clothes were hung in the closet, and there was a cold bottle of champagne on a table in the bedroom with a balcony that overlooked the city. Next to the champagne bottle was a note, explaining that I would meet Meyer in his private office at one in the afternoon the next day.

I looked through the closet. Everything had been cleaned and pressed. The pants still fit comfortably, but the jackets and sport coats were too small. For several years I'd been doing pull-ups from the bars on my cell window and push-ups on the floor. I was a half inch bigger across the chest. I stood in front of a full-length mirror and tried on a suit coat. My added size made the sleeves ride up. I held my arms up from my sides with my elbows bent and brought my arms and shoulders forward until the seam of the coat ripped. It made me smile.

The following day I arrived ten minutes early at Hôtel Ritz for my meeting with Meyer Lacombe. The faint scent of lilac and lavender wafted through the lobby. The young woman just inside the entryway had been replaced by a blonde. She too was dressed in blue livery. The woman at the head of the stairs—again dressed in a white blouse, red skirt, and heels—was a younger version than the last, or maybe she was the same but hadn't aged. I ascended the stairs and was shown into Meyer's office.

Meyer was seated at a table near the balcony. The table was laid with a white cloth and set for lunch. When he saw me, he stood. I watched him. *How had he so easily imprisoned and then released me?* I wondered. *Money, corruption, blackmail, the gossamer of power held by the invisible?*

"Nicholas, please join me."

I took a seat at the table, and he poured me a glass of wine. The glass was in a patch of sunlight on the white cloth. The wine was dark cherry in color.

"You're looking well." He wasn't looking at me when he said this; his attention was with the cork as he replaced it in the bottle. He had aged little, while I had gained ten years in appearance. The anger in my heart was controlled.

He removed a silver cover from a serving plate on the table and invited me to help myself. There were sandwiches of thinly sliced venison with sweet horseradish on crusty bread. I opened a sandwich and picked through it with a knife and fork. I ate just the venison. Meat was a luxury I hadn't had in five years.

"I have a task for you," he said.

There was no need to insult me with small talk, a history of my past years. The task was the only reason I was out of prison. Nor had my imprisonment been a prerequisite to the task he was about to reveal, the nature of which had been decided upon years ago. I was an afterthought, a disposable item to its accomplishment. *Oh yes, that silly boy, the social climber, poking his nose into my life—we'll use him. Yes, I'd forgotten about him. He'll do…quite disposable.*

"Nine million dollars," Meyer said. "US dollars. Does that sound familiar? I'm sure it does. The money is in a bank in Hong Kong, an English bank. No longer in Quebec." He placed a leather-bound notepad on the table. "Here are the account numbers and pass codes. It's under your name. Your new name."

He placed a passport on the ledger.

I opened it…and read.

I looked up. "Firthwhile…Nicholas Firthwhile?"

"Yes, you wish to be part of the patrician class. I've created it for you. I'm sure your father-in-law—your *former* father-in-law—would approve."

"Was his death natural?"

He cut a small sandwich in half.

"Politics are essential to our species, Nicholas. The palace eunuchs of the great dynasties of China were more powerful than the emperor. If one of them threatened the privileges of the group, he was done away with. Would you care for more venison?"

I shook my head. "No, thank you."

When Meyer had finished chewing, he said, "When you arrive in your hotel room tomorrow in London, you'll find a weapon, with instructions and an address. You'll use this weapon to kill John Savensworth." He refilled his wineglass. "From there you'll travel to Hong Kong and collect your reward. As long as you don't return to Europe, you'll not be bothered."

He pushed his chair out from the table.

"Now if you'll excuse me."

I traveled from Paris to Coquelles, where I boarded the tunnel train for Folkestone and then continued to London. My room was at the Berkeley on Wilton Place, near Wilton Crescent. I don't believe the proximity to the home of the late Lord Nigel Firth—now owned by Adrienne—was a coincidence, but running into Nigel's widow was.

My reservation had been made under the name Nicholas Firthwhile. Being referred to as Mr. Firthwhile had a pleasing sound. It seemed I had slipped into my new identity as though it were new skin.

In my room I found a bottle of champagne in an ice bucket with a note next to it: "With sincere hope your bed is to your liking." I dropped the note and looked under the mattress, where I found a 9 mm pistol with a silencer along with a note with an address. John Savensworth was in London to see Pamela. He was staying at a private residence in Belgravia, sublet for his convenience.

The task in front of me seemed impossible. I liked John. I liked him very much. He was sincere, unaffected, with a nature incapable of harming another creature. But if I didn't carry out Meyer's "request," I'd be eliminated. I had no doubt.

None.

At first I thought I could disappear somewhere into the third world, assume yet another identity, but the thought of living as a beggar in some hovel in the slums of Rio or in some isolated wilderness away from all society was unbearable. I might find the behavior of humans repugnant, but I need them in view. A cruel irony.

I removed the pistol and attached the silencer. There was a fully loaded clip next to it. I inserted the clip, pushed it in place, and aimed toward the window.

What choice did I have?

The next morning I went for an early walk and stopped for coffee at Starbucks. The air was chilly, even damp, but I sat outside. I noticed a woman coming toward me along the sidewalk, and for a moment, I thought it was Adrienne. I called to her. She stopped and looked at me. Her expression was questioning: perhaps she knew me, perhaps she didn't.

Then I realized it was Carolyn.

"It's Nick," I said, as she still looked puzzled.

"Oh my gosh! Nicholas!" She came forward with her hand out. "I thought you were in prison?"

"The ruling—my sentence, that is—was overturned."

I could see that she didn't believe me, but she had the decency not to pursue it.

"Adrienne isn't here. She moved to South Africa. She lives in Durban now."

"I heard."

"Her grandmother died. Left everything to her. *Everything*," she emphasized. She stared at me for a moment. "She's a wealthy woman now. You should look her up. You're still married, right?"

"I believe so. How are you?"

"Nigel didn't leave me much. But I get along. Maybe you could talk to Adrienne? She has her father's money. Ninety percent of it. It seems I should have gotten more. I was his wife, and she—well... did you know about them?" She stared at me. "I heard them in the bedroom together...laughing. Then it got very quiet. Is that why she got all the money?" There was shame, or outrage, or both in her expression. Then she suddenly seemed embarrassed and said she had to go.

"It was nice seeing you," she said. "Tell Adrienne...tell her I said hello. But don't repeat..." She ran off.

She crossed the street and walked quickly in the other direction. Within a moment she had turned another corner and was gone. I sat back down at my table and stared at the corner where she had only moments ago turned and disappeared.

It was a Thursday night, and John Savensworth was at his sublet flat in London. Pamela had come down from the castle in Scotland to spend a long weekend with her father. They were going to go out to dinner and then attend a new art gallery presenting the works of an artist Pamela described as a real genius. "You've got to see his work! It's so good you can't understand it. But that's why he's a genius." John didn't care for theaters or art galleries, but to see his daughter enjoy herself was all he wanted. Her happiness.

Meyer was alone at his London residence that night. Tziporah was out. She might be gone for an hour at the most, she'd written on a note left on Meyer's desk in his downstairs study. The note was at the very edge of the desk. Against the dark polish of the teakwood, it was easily seen.

I was dressed in dark clothes—an open collar and a navy blazer. I inserted the pistol under my belt and buttoned the blazer. I wore black calfskin gloves.

Pamela and her father had returned from the art gallery by 11:00 p.m. I arrived at Meyer's study at 11:45 p.m. I let myself in through the glass doors that looked out onto the garden. I saw Meyer standing in front of the fireplace. He had just lit a cigar and threw the match into the open fire. He turned when he heard the patio doors open.

"What are you doing here?" he asked. His usual calm was gone. "You should be at Heathrow by now. Are you crazy?"

"I have to first earn my keep. My nine million. My release from prison."

I removed the pistol from my belt and stepped closer to Meyer. The silencer was inches from his forehead. His eyes got big.

"Good," I said. "You understand."

INSIGHT

If I had killed John Savensworth, it might have guaranteed a wealthy life, but Meyer had said to me during our first meeting, "The ability to gather information and, from that information, create new information is a rare talent." I had gathered a great deal of information regarding the history of Meyer Lacombe, the most potent of which was the dominant force that Tziporah held in his life. Once I'd lived up to my end of Meyer's bargain, he might have allowed me to live. But not Tziporah. She knew intuitively that all bargains mutate under the pressure of self-preservation, and 99 percent of all mutations are fatal to the organism—in this case the bargain, Meyer's bargain—and Tziporah wasn't a gambler.

Before my flight had landed in Hong Kong, Tziporah would have found Meyer lying on the floor of his study. For an instant she would have felt confused, startled, stunned...*Why is he lying there, facedown?*

My God, blood!

Her heart racing, pounding in her chest.

So much blood...no...it couldn't be.

It can't be.

Rushing to him, kneeling in the blood, trying to move him. Nothing. Deadweight.

Oh my God, no!

Thirty minutes after I'd left Meyer lying in his own blood—driving to Heathrow in a rented car, headlights coming toward me from the opposite direction—I realized I'd killed the wrong one.

Tziporah!

LAYONNA

I boarded Swiss Air flight ninety-nine from Heathrow to Hong Kong with one stop in Zurich. I was seated in first class. I had one piece of luggage, a carry-on that I stowed above my seat. We were still on the tarmac, waiting to be pushed away from the boarding area. The stewardess asked if I cared for something to drink.

I stared at her without answering.

After a moment she said, "Are you OK?"

"Yes." I hesitated. "I'm fine."

I thought for a moment, trying to put my thoughts together. *She'd said something about a drink.*

"Vodka," I said, but I wasn't a vodka drinker. Why did I say that?

"How would you like it?"

I stared at her.

"How would you like it?" she repeated.

"With ice."

She started to turn away.

"A double, please."

She looked back at me. "Are you sure you're OK? Did you bang yourself?"

"Excuse me...?"

"Your forehead."

"Forehead?" I touched my forehead with my fingertips. I felt something crusty. "I don't know," I said. "Where's—"

"Right here. Through the folding door."

I pushed the doors open to the tiny restroom. The light came on. I looked in the mirror. At first I thought they were tiny scabs across my forehead, but it was dried blood. *Blood spatter.* I soaked a paper towel with water, cleaned my face, and dried it.

Jesus Christ! I came through the check-in like this.

I checked the front of my blazer. There was blood spatter on the sleeves. I cleaned them thoroughly with wet paper towels. Then I flushed the towels.

What else had I forgotten?

I remembered having thrown the gloves into a trash bin and had a cloudy remembrance of having tossed the 9 mm into the Thames. *But what else...what did I forget?*

When I returned to my seat, the stewardess arrived a moment later with my drink.

"Feeling better?" she asked.

"Yes, thank you."

I took a large swallow of the vodka.

I had learned about muscle relaxers from Adrienne, and when I'd arrived in London from Paris, it was one of the first things I'd obtained from the chemist's shop. I took one from my inside blazer pocket and swallowed it with the rest of the vodka. By the time we were lifting off the runway into the air, I felt the sweet tingling of the carisoprodol throughout my body as I slipped away into sleep.

I was holding a falcon—or was it an eagle?—in both hands, holding it out from me. I released my hands to watch the bird take flight. But it didn't. Before dropping to the ground, the raptor turned into a child and landed on both feet and then started to grow. I watched with curiosity: how much power, thrust must the woman-child generate with her human wings to overcome the weight of her own body, to take flight? To fly? I tried to work it out: I erased the equation from the whiteboard in my dream and started over.

"Lord Firthwhile, we're preparing to land. Tray in the upright position, please."

A female voice announced over the intercom that if any passenger wished to leave the plane, "Please take your boarding pass. We depart again in thirty minutes."

Once we were on the ground, I asked the stewardess for another drink. "The same...Thank you. A double."

She returned with the vodka. I took another carisoprodol from my inside pocket and swallowed it with the vodka. Moments later the stewardess covered me with a blanket. She placed it over my lap and over one shoulder. From my peripheral view, I glimpsed her look of pity. Or was it sympathy? I slipped into tingly oblivion.

I heard the muffled sound of jet engines and raised the window shade to see the faint pearly light of dawn across a distant horizon. I sat up straight, felt stiffness in my back. The stewardess noticed I had come around.

"You slept the whole way," she said. "Coffee?"

"Thank you."

As she stepped away, I noticed the young woman across the aisle from me with blondish hair. She looked straight at me. Dark eyes. White teeth. She wore a skirt, stockings, and red shoes. *She must have boarded in Zurich.*

I turned back to the oval window and looked out. Turbulence suddenly struck the cabin. Over the intercom a female voice asked everyone to make sure their seat belts were fastened. I held my coffee up from the fold-down tray. Another surge of turbulence. The young woman across the aisle was standing. She opened the storage bin above her seat.

"Miss, please take your seat," the stewardess said.

"I can't find my purse."

"I'll help you but not at this moment. Please."

Another surge of turbulence, and the young woman lost her balance and fell to the floor. The blanket she had moved fell from the storage bin and now covered her head. The stewardess held herself tightly against the turbulence. From under the blanket, the young woman tried to free herself. Once she had the blanket off her head, she looked around with her hair covering her face. The stewardess bent forward to help her.

"Please, miss…"

"Oh, look," the young woman said. "There…My purse…"

The stewardess picked it up and handed it to her. "Is this it?"

"It has my name on it. See?"

Across the front of the leather bag were raised letters: "Pamela Savensworth." She pointed to the letters.

"That's me," she said, as if the name would cause instant recognition.

The stewardess said, "That's fine, but please remain seated while the cabin is made ready for landing." Young Savensworth looked toward me, her finger still pointing to her name. I smiled, turned, and looked out the oval window.

Jesus Christ! How did this happen?

As the airplane entered a steep bank over the water, I saw Hong Kong International Airport in the distance. Beyond the airport were the mountains and the great land of China.

How did she end up on this flight? She has no idea who I am—how could she?

The English community is large enough to remain inconspicuous.

Even so, I need to avoid her.

Once we had landed, and it was safe to gather our things, I quickly removed my carry-on bag from the overhead compartment and entered the aisle to leave the plane. I made an effort not to look at Pamela but then turned for a quick peek. She was staring at me.

"Sorry," she said. "Didn't mean to stare." She crinkled her nose. "Guess I got caught."

I smiled.

"You stand out," she said. "I mean, you look so different."

I didn't want to get into a conversation, so I nodded and said nothing.

Several moments went by while we were waiting in line to exit the plane.

"You here for a visit?" she asked.

If I had answered, it would have sounded as if I wanted conversation, so I just shook my head and looked straight ahead.

"I'm on holiday," she said. "Mother said, 'Go somewhere, please. Anywhere. China.' So I bought a ticket to Hong Kong. Have you been here before?"

Again I shook my head, thinking, *I can't believe this shit—her father is so nice, and she can't keep her mouth shut.*

"She just wanted to get rid of me. Said I was underfoot. Should've gone to see Father instead. He lives in America. Maryland, actually. You look American."

I didn't say anything.

"Where are you staying?"

Without looking at her, I said, "Can't remember. I have it written down somewhere."

"I don't have a reservation. I just left. Guess I didn't give it much thought. Where'd you say you're staying?"

"Once in the terminal," I said, "you'll find a place to stay. They're listed."

"If you don't mind, I'll just go where you're going. Then I won't have to think about it."

Holy shit!

When we were inside the terminal, she offered her hand. "I'm Pamela."

I took her hand. "Nice to meet you."

I tried to release her hand, but she held on. "And you are?"

"Nicholas. Nicholas Firthwhile."

"Sounds so formal. Nicholas. Is that what everyone calls you—Nicholas?" she asked, turning her head to look around. "Where do we get our luggage?"

Pamela found an attendant and asked for directions to the luggage claim. As she stepped away, I thought this was the perfect time to disappear, but I didn't move. The first of my many mistakes with her. She gathered her bags, and the attendant stacked them on a pushcart. On the way to the taxi stand, I glimpsed the name of a hotel on an electronic advertising board. It proclaimed to be a luxury hotel, far above the noise of Hong Kong.

Once her bags were in the cab, I said to the driver, "Dragonfly Towers."

"Oh," Pamela said, sliding into the backseat of the cab. "Sounds like fun. Dragonflies."

Layonna was a daughter of the East, the water, the tropics. Her complexion wasn't Asian, white, or Polynesian. She was all of this. The oral history conveyed to her from childhood begins with Ashar Bajwa, a Sikh of Indian origin.

Ashar Bajwa arrived in Hong Kong at the time the United Kingdom hoisted its flag above the port city in 1841. For a time Ashar felt he had broken free of his background, his caste, by taking a surname of the Jatt. After he joined the British military, he distinguished himself through his ingenuity and agility and soon acquired the rank of honorary officer. His abilities and the favor with which the British officers viewed him, however, created jealousy and suspicion as to Ashar's true background.

When the story was created by his rivals that he was of a much-lower caste than his name suggested, the rumors and gossip took on a life of their own. Members of the Indian military agreed that Ashar was a fraud and was actually of the lowest caste possible. This caused discomfort for the British military. How can a man lead when he's looked upon as an untouchable? Ashar Bajwa was subsequently expelled from the military.

Penniless and living among the estuaries of Hong Kong, he came across a sampan drifting in the backwaters of the harbor. For several days he waited to see whether it was claimed. Then one night in a heavy rain, he took refuge under its bamboo-and-wicker roof. As time passed, Ashar assumed the sampan was a gift from God.

Ashar's wife, Chu Tee, was Tanka—a Chinese boat dweller, a sea gypsy, a person thought to be of lesser being than a homeless peasant, an untouchable. Ashar had purchased Chu Tee for three baskets of fish before she'd reached puberty; she had been fathered by a Portuguese sailor who had taken a Tanka woman for his concubine and then discarded her. For many generations to come, the sampan was home for the descendants of Ashar Bajwa and Chu Tee.

The mysticism, Layonna said, was the continuity of white, Indian, and Asian blood through the coming generations, as if the universe had decided the direction of her ancestry: a Chinese woman had been raped by British soldiers, and now an outcast by her own people, she was taken in by the sea gypsies. Her son then married into the Bajwa clan. Later the boat people of Indian blood, a tribe unto themselves, mixed with the Tanka, while on the perimeter, the blood of the British occasionally found its way into the moonlight.

Through the years the sampan periodically was taken into the backwaters, the estuaries of its origin, for refurbishment. At one point, after much saving, patience, and scavenging, a sail was added, which made available the deeper waters of larger fish.

There were times of abundance, scarcity, typhoons, disasters, death, and marriages. Through it all the progeny of Ashar Bajwa remained on the water. It was their home, their place of survival and safety. Only rarely did a member, a gypsy of the Bajwa, leave the water for land. For this person, man or woman, tragedy often followed, for the Bajwa believed God had given the sampan for them to live on the water, upon the ocean, mother of all life.

Do not turn your back on your mother.

D ragonfly Towers faced the waters of Victoria Harbor and Hong Kong Island. Modern pleasure yachts, commercial ships of industry, and smaller boats of labor dotted the waters. In the distance, thin clouds stretched along the morning horizon above the still ocean. In the opposite direction was the ancient land of China, the view obstructed by low mountains.

The hotel lobby was made of chrome and glass, with white marble floors. Tropical plants adorned the near-sterile environment to create a fairyland of the future, while indoor ponds and aquariums created a sense of serenity.

Pamela's bags were brought into the lobby as she looked about, smiling as though she were about to step through the looking glass to the other side.

"We have no reservations," I explained at the front counter.

"This is no problem, Lord Firthwhile." The transition from West to East arrives with politeness, a slight bow of the head, eager courtesy. "We shall accommodate your every need."

Lacombe & Lacombe owned a suite of high-rise rooms in Hong Kong, but Pamela didn't know this. She knew no more about her uncle's life outside of Scotland or London than a teenager knows of politics. She now occupied a two-bedroom suite one floor above the man who, hours ago, had killed her beloved uncle Meyer.

My rooms were on the eighteenth floor and faced Victoria Harbor. The wall that faced the water was all glass. Pamela's suite was at the other end on the nineteenth floor and also faced the harbor.

Once I had checked in and was in my suite, I felt exhausted even though I'd slept most of the time on the plane. I wanted a drink and more muscle relaxers, but instead I changed into my running shorts and shoes. When I saw the few things in my bag, I decided I'd go shopping the next day. And then the bank: $9 million. Or was it all a ruse?

The leather-bound notepad with the account numbers and pass codes was in my bag. I opened it and looked through the pages. What if the money didn't exist? I sat down on the edge of the bed. What then?

But for now I needed fresh oxygen in my brain, my muscles. The fitness center was on the fifth floor.

Inside the elevator I pushed the "down" button, but the elevator went up and stopped at nineteenth floor. The door opened, and Pamela was standing there.

"Hi." She crinkled her nose. "Going to the fitness center? Cute shorts."

"Yes."

"Great idea. Let me change." She held the elevator door with her hand. "I'll meet you there." The doors closed.

Jesus Christ!

I was on the treadmill when she arrived in the fitness center. I saw her through the glass doors. Her gym suit was skintight, with bare skin from her breast line to belly button. The halter top was red and also tight fitting over her full breasts. She had her mother's figure. She stepped on the treadmill next to me and started pushing buttons while things beeped and flashed red and green.

"How does this thing work?" she asked me.

"Push 'start.'"

"I did. Nothing happened."

I stepped off the treadmill and set the program for her.

"Oh," she said. "Now I get it." A moment later, as she walked in place, she said, "My mother sent a bodyguard to watch me."

"A what?"

"A bodyguard. Mohammed something or other. He's in the hotel. I saw him. On your floor, actually."

I pushed the "stop" button and walked to a standstill on the treadmill while looking at her.

"According to Mother I'm part something or other too. Do you think so? Do I look Arab? I think I look like my father."

I agreed, but I could hardly tell her I knew him. "A bodyguard?"

"You sound surprised. She and Uncle Meyer worry about me. Well, not her as much as Uncle Meyer. He's pretty sweet—he really is." She pushed the speed button several times to make the treadmill go faster. "I'm not even out of breath," she said. "Pretty good, eh?"

She noticed me staring at her.

"Are you finished?" she asked.

"No," I said. "No, I'm just curious about the bodyguard."

She started to breathe a little harder.

"I don't think Mother did it. She's not like that. You know, thoughtful. It was Uncle Meyer, I'm sure. He's like a second father to me. Always has been. He used to play with me and organize birthday parties for me. They were really something—like the circus had come to town."

"Have you talked to your mother?"

"No…" Beads of perspiration ran from her face, down her throat, her chest, between her breasts. "No, I called Uncle Meyer…" She was short of breath. "I left a voice mail."

Layonna first appeared as a passing shadow at the edge of my vision. I glimpsed her for but a moment in the hotel lobby— her autumn-like presence amid tropical plants. I stepped around the floor plants—urns and vases filled with flowers and ferns— to see her again. She walked toward an atrium-like lounge with glass-topped tables and cushioned chairs and then disappeared through the service doors.

I took a seat near an indoor pond filled with orange-and-black fish, their fins like long plumes, underwater flowers. I sat there feeling slightly foolish. Who was she? Where had she gone?

A young woman approached, petite, polite. "Someone will be with you in a moment." She bowed in a subtle gesture.

Minutes later Layonna appeared in the attire of a waitress.

"May I help you?"

Her hair was black but not shiny, worn in a lose bun with long strands falling free. There was no curl to her hair. A white comb held it loosely together. Above her dark eyes, a faint line defined her eyelids. Her complexion was ivory; her lips were moist, and her teeth were white as her lips parted in a smile. This wasn't the beauty of *Glamour, Vogue,* or *Playboy;* this was heart stopping.

"Yes," I said, staring at her.

"You wish a lunch menu?"

"No. I'll have a glass of champagne. And a croissant. Do you have croissants?"

"Yes." She smiled as though she were aware of something I was not.

Minutes later she returned with champagne in a tall flute and a warm croissant on a white plate. Next to the croissant were three strawberries with green stems.

"You wish something else?" she asked.

Her eyebrows were beautifully arched, and she wore no lipstick, yet her lips were darker than her complexion. When she smiled it came slowly, her teeth appearing white and moist. I felt a sinking in my chest.

"Thank you," I said, "for the strawberries."

"They come with the champagne. Do you wish more of me?"

A sip of champagne went the wrong way—I coughed. "Excuse me?"

She smiled. "From our lunch menu…"

I shook my head. "No…thank you…very much."

She turned to leave but then stopped. She turned back to me. "Are you staying here?"

"Here…ha…yes." My heart was racing. "Here in the hotel?"

"Then we'll meet again, yes?" She smiled. "I'm Layonna."

"Layonna…" I repeated.

She pointed to her name tag, and then, very slightly, she tilted her head as if to say, *And your name…?*

"Oh yes. Sorry. Nicholas. Nicholas Firthwhile." At that moment my new name seemed to be part of me, who I had become. It fit with the same pleasure as the tuxedo Peterus had tailored for me. I had become the creation of Meyer Lacombe.

Before leaving she looked at me again. "You are striking to see," she said. "So different."

⊷ ⊶

As I left the hotel—my head light with champagne—I realized I might very well be a pauper.

Penniless.

My very next thought was of Layonna. But I had no time for that now. Without money there's no time for anything.

Meyer had referred to a Canadian bank, but the money was supposedly in the Royal Bank of Hong Kong, and I had no idea how China had changed the rules. It was now "their" island, their city.

The Royal Bank of Hong Kong—that was all that mattered at the moment. But as I soon learned, it was the Royal Bank of Scotland in Hong Kong. I don't believe that was a mistake on Meyer's part. So when Mr. Gui of the Royal Bank of Scotland politely informed me that the account I inquired about had been moved to Deutsche Bank in Hong Kong, I was relieved to know the account actually existed and frightened that it might also prove to be another "envelope of ashes."

Deutsche Bank in Hong Kong is at 1 Austin Road, Kowloon, on the fifty-second floor. From such a height, the Hong Kong of glass-and-chrome skyscrapers is modern to the eye and mind, but from street level, your insignificance is thrown in your face. Everything is compacted into small, singular spaces. An ancient culture that has never practiced the idea of the "individual" doesn't understand the idea.

Mr. Gui had referred me to Mr. Boquin, and upon my inquiry, and very polite reception at the Deutsche Bank, I was escorted to a waiting area. The sofa and chairs were covered in white leather stretched skintight, the end tables were metal and glass, the floor was stone, and the walls were dark gray and white. The artwork on the walls and the few sculptures on the glass tables were without lines or warmth. Above the sofa a large painting on white canvas had several brushstrokes in black with a gray shadow and a splatter of red in the corner as though it were a warning. I sat on the sofa and waited, my back to the painting.

I was soon greeted by a young woman in a dark suit, heels, and sheer stockings. She smiled, introduced herself, and led me to an office door down the hall. As I entered the office, it seemed as though I had stepped through a porthole back into Europe.

Mr. Boquin stood in the middle of the carpeted office. He offered his hand and welcomed me. He was young, maybe thirty, with unmanageable porcupine hair. Behind him was a view of Victoria Harbor, the island of Hong Kong, and the distant ocean. The carpeting he stood upon was Persian, and the walls were covered in a rich paneling, lined with leather-bound books. The oversize desk in front of the window appeared handcrafted and made of African bloodwood.

To my right was another door, nearly camouflaged against the paneling. The door opened, and a man with blondish hair emerged. As he stepped closer, I saw his gray eyes and practiced smile. He introduced himself as Hans Freidman.

"Mr. Firthwhile, I've been expecting you." His English was flawless, yet I detected a faint German accent. "Please sit down. May I offer you a drink? Sherry?"

"Yes, I'd like that."

Mr. Boquin and the young woman were gone. I heard the door close behind me.

Hans Freidman handed me the glass of sherry. He looked at me for a moment without speaking, considering a thought perhaps, a description, or a profile of me he'd read. It was unnerving.

"I must admit you're a mystery to me," he said. "I wasn't given much information. Just a set of instructions."

He didn't take a seat behind his desk but in a leather reading chair near a floor lamp. With his open hand, he offered the chair next to his. The light from the lamp above us was soft pink.

"The American Express card you've been using," he said, "will soon expire."

Here it comes, I thought.

"We'll provide you with a debit card. As for the funds, well, they've diminished somewhat. But very little. In the scheme of things, that is."

So far so good.

He noticed I'd finished my drink rather quickly.

"Care for another?" he asked, with just the touch of a smile.

Or was it a smirk?

"Thank you," I said.

He poured another drink, handed it to me, and sat back down in his chair. He said nothing at first, as if considering his words carefully, and then again offered the slight smile. Was he amused by my discomfort, my apprehension?

"The funds were transferred from the Royal Bank of Canada to China Construction Bank. In Beijing. For cleansing purposes, you might say." He shifted his weight in the leather chair.

"It's still a great deal of money," he continued. "Nine million dollars. A private account that size may draw attention. So we advise you invest it. Turn it into stockholdings. Real and otherwise. For that purpose Heinrich Eichmann will assist you. Dividends and such—on a titular level—will transfer to the Royal Bank of Scotland. This will give a satisfying appearance for tax purposes."

He finished by taking a sip of his drink, and then, as if considering another thought, went to his desk. He picked up the phone and pushed the intercom button. "*Bitte senden Sie Herr Eichmann in mein Büro.*"

He turned to me. "I'll introduce you to Herr Heinrich Eichmann. He's very capable."

Herr Eichmann was in his late twenties and had a serious smile (if you could call it a smile), and as I soon learned, he lived in a world of numbers, projections, and calculations and had a low tolerance for anything out of place, whether it was a pencil or a paper clip, and treated his spreadsheets with the same intolerance for error. He already had created a plan of investment, diversified, and spread out across the globe. As he explained his strategy in detail, I nodded as if I understood every word, but I'd lost track of his explanation early on.

I don't think people mattered much to Eichmann. They were too unpredictable. Numbers had an absolute value. People were the reason the markets went up and down. His penchant for numbers and his intolerance for human behavior were why I trusted him.

Within a few days I received a debit card and a credit card. The debit card was drawn on the Construction Bank of China and the credit card on the Royal Bank of Scotland. Eichmann forwarded all the necessary information so I could access my account online, while the passwords he delivered in person.

My anxiety, it seemed, had been for nothing. I wasn't vastly wealthy, but at the present, as I sat on the sofa in my suite, looking out at Victoria Harbor, I was indeed well-off.

Meyer had kept his part of the bargain...and then I thought of what I had done.

From the lobby I saw a cab pull up to the front doors of the hotel. The driver got out and opened the rear passenger door. Pamela emerged with several shopping bags. The cab driver removed a few boxes from the trunk and followed her into the lobby. When she saw me, her face lit up.

"Guess what? I thought of the perfect name for you."

Her ability to assume familiarity with a near stranger was astounding.

"*Nicky.*" She looked at me for a moment. "What do you think? It's better than"—she lowered her voice—"Nicholas."

"I don't know," I said. Coming from someone other than Adrienne, it didn't sound right. From Adrienne it was maternal, incestuous, loving, caring, sexual.

"You don't *know?*"

Her feelings were hurt. It was the first time I saw her pout—the lower lip coming out and chin dimpled—but not the last time. I ignored it and said I was on my way out.

"Out? Where're you going?"

"Shopping," I said and soon realized it was a mistake to have used the word *shopping*.

"Oh! I'll come with you."

I didn't answer.

"Unless you don't want me around…" The lower lip came out.

I had planned on visiting a tailor. I'd gotten the name from the concierge service for the suites owned by Lacombe & Lacombe and worried Pamela might recognize something. Nor did I want to listen to her constant flow of naïveté.

"You might find it boring," I said.

"Let me worry about that." Her smile was warm and open, her teeth beautifully white, healthy. She took my arm in hers. "I already have a cab. See? You need me."

Her hip brushed against me and then pressed against my leg, and I suddenly was aware of her adult femininity and the sweet airy scent of her perfume—English perfume.

The tailor shop was on Austin Road, and the tailor was in his early forties and was originally from Shanghai. While in his shop, I glimpsed him a few times in the back at the cutting table and at a sewing machine. His wife took my order and measurements. Her English was good, although halting. She was originally from Beijing. She recorded my measurements in a notebook, with a very neat, precise hand, and then reassured me everything would go into the computer.

Pamela paged through a magazine of men's fashions, while I ordered several pairs of slacks, a sport coat, and a half dozen shirts.

"Look," Pamela said, "you have to get this."

She pointed to a page in the magazine, but I couldn't see the picture.

"This," she said, her finger still on the picture. "A tuxedo. Then take me out to dinner. Someplace special."

After a few more stops for shoes, belts, underwear—a few ready-made items—we arrived back at the hotel. From inside the lobby, I thought I saw Layonna near the atrium lounge.

"We have to have a practice," Pamela said.

"Practice?" I was still looking toward the atrium.

"A practice dinner. Before the special one. Pick me up at eight. No…seven. That's better."

I looked at her. *What the hell is she talking about?*

"See me up to my room," she said.

She had me by the arm again. The now-familiar hip against my leg but more obvious. We took the elevator up to the nineteenth floor. I stopped at her door. I wasn't about to go in. She opened the door with her keycard.

"Come in," she said.

I glanced at my watch. "Really don't have time. I'll see you at—"

"Seven." She crinkled her nose.

I took the stairs down to my suite on the eighteenth floor. As I stood at my door with the keycard in hand, a man down the hall, Middle Eastern in appearance, inserted his keycard into his door lock while staring at me. He held my eyes for several long moments as if frozen in motion. I opened my door and went inside.

I had a strong hunch who it was, and I wanted to think he was just "flirting" with me. But he wasn't.

⊷⊶

I wore the blazer I had worn the night I'd left London. I'd had it cleaned the morning I'd gotten here. My shirt was open at the neck.

I tapped on Pamela's door. She opened it immediately. She wore a black dress with a low neckline, her cleavage well displayed. Her smile was open and happy. As she stepped forward, the hall light caught her eyes, a glint of dark crystal.

She brushed something from my lapel. "You wore that on the plane, didn't you?"

I didn't answer.

The Dragonfly Restaurant was on the twenty-eighth floor. Our table was near the window and covered with a white cloth. The stemware was paper thin and had a pleasing "ting." Through the window, the tall buildings, skyscrapers of glass against the night, were a prism of light.

Our waiter pushed a cart with champagne on ice to the table. He filled Pamela's glass. She raised the tall flute to her lips. "You have to see my room," she said and then sipped the wine. "I changed the bedroom. They had everything in the wrong place. You have to see it. After dinner. Promise?"

I smiled.

She then talked about the view, her shopping trip, and mentioned she hadn't yet called her mother to tell her where she was.

"After all, she told me, 'Take a trip. Anywhere! Go to China.' Won't she be surprised? Hong Kong. And look how beautiful it is." She gestured toward the night with her champagne glass and then stopped and looked at me. "But she already knows, doesn't she? Mohammed's here. Are you hungry?" she asked. "Where's our waiter?"

Pamela ordered lobster, and I ordered a salad with a few pieces of shrimp. She continued to talk about one thing after another, while my thoughts lingered on the memory of Layonna's face. She was like a melody that played over and over in my thoughts.

I noticed that our waiter had received a word or two from the maître d' and that he now looked toward our table and then came forward. He excused himself for interrupting and said Pamela had a phone call.

"A phone call? How exciting," she said. "Like one of those old movies—in black and white—where the waiter always comes to the table, because no one has a mobile yet, and says to, like, Ingrid Bergman or someone, 'You have a phone call, madam.'"

While getting to her feet, she took a small piece of lobster tail with her fingers, dipped it in the butter, and put it in her mouth.

"That's so good," she said and then sucked her thumb and finger clean.

As she started to walk away, I offered her a napkin. "Here," I said.

She stopped. "Oh…isn't that sweet of you? Thank you."

She wiped her fingers and then her mouth, leaving lipstick on the white napkin, and then dropped it on the table.

While she was gone, my curiosity grew: who would know to call her here? Several minutes passed, and then a few more.

As Pamela returned, as she walked toward our table, she looked dazed. She sat down, the color drained from her face.

"What's wrong?"

"You won't believe this," she said. "I don't…"

I had a suspicion. "What is it?"

"Uncle Meyer's dead. Someone killed him."

I took a long drink of champagne, my eyes watching her over the top of my glass, waiting.

"Who…?" she said, still with a stunned look. "Who could've done such a thing?"

Before I'd been sent to prison, I'd had dinner on several occasions with John Savensworth. Our reservations were almost always in the hotel dining room, elegant and warm with soft lighting. At first John asked whether formal attire was required. After a small hesitation, I smiled and said yes. He smiled too. We were both partial to tuxedos. He had grown up in the oil fields of Texas, and I'd grown up in Detroit. Owning a tuxedo was a symbol of success, an acceptance to another class.

After Tziporah's departure from Texas, John seldom spoke of her. I don't believe it was due to any special dislike; his work had replaced her. But not so with Pamela—he adored his daughter, while Meyer had managed one roadblock after another to limit John's time with her. It seemed there was always a trip of some kind, a special camp for young girls or a visit with a distant relative that interfered with any plans Pamela might have had to see her father, most certainly if the plans involved traveling to America, which Tziporah hated.

"I knew what he was doing," John had said of Meyer. "All the excuses why Pamela couldn't come. If I suggested I'd come to Europe, Tziporah made excuses. Said they were leaving to go on holiday—or whatever."

He motioned to the waiter, indicating his glass. A few minutes later, the waiter brought him another glass of bourbon.

"I didn't have the stomach to fight about it," he said. "Anyway, I felt sorry for Meyer. He's sterile—shooting blanks. Pamela's the closest he'd come to having a daughter. But still"—he looked at me, the bourbon glass in his hand—"it hurt."

I was drinking champagne, and before John's steak arrived, he'd finished three bourbons and become even more talkative.

"Meyer once asked me to go with him. Said he had a chore, or maybe it was an errand. Something like that…I don't remember exactly. So I went with him. When we got into the car, I thought I smelled fried chicken. I looked around…but nothing.

"Anyway, he started driving as if he were leaving the city. It was dark, and he followed the river. The moon was just a faint sliver, with almost no stars. For a moment I had this thought—*What if he wants to get rid of me? Dump my body in the river?* Sounds crazy, I know. But if I were gone, he'd become Pamela's de facto father. But that wasn't the case—obviously. Anyway, I don't think Meyer has ever wished me harm. He might be jealous, but that's the extent of it. I'm sure of that."

A cart was pushed to our table, and John's steak was uncovered and placed in front of him. Next to the steak lay a thin carrot and a spear of broccoli. I had a green salad with a piece of salmon placed in the center. The waiter refilled my wineglass.

John poured a teaspoon of salt into the palm of his hand and, with his thumb and finger, sprinkled salt over his steak. When he finished, he still had salt in the palm of his hand. He looked around as if trying to decide what to do with it and then let his hand slip to his side and brushed the salt to the carpet.

He cut a small piece of steak, using his knife and fork English style, and tasted it.

He nodded while chewing. "Not Texas but good."

He put the napkin to his lips and looked at me. "That smell—in the car—it *was* chicken after all. Meyer pulled into a path that led down to the river. Ahead of us I saw a fire. A small fire for warming hands. Well, there were half dozen men around the fire. Homeless men. They looked as if they hadn't bathed in weeks. And there was a dog. It broke my heart to see the dog. But he seemed happy. He lay near the fire and wagged his tail.

"Meyer stops the car and gets out. You could see they all knew him. One guy says, ''Ello cap'in' in that cockney sound. People say Texans have an accent—personally I don't think so; at least I've never heard it.

"Anyway, Meyer opens the trunk and takes out these white boxes, full of chicken, and what they call 'chips' (nothing but French fries), and hands them out. Then he hands a big piece of chicken to the dog. Most people would just throw it to the dog. But he handed it to him.

"One of the men says, 'I thank ya, cap'in. My-tee fine a'ya. My-tee fine...'" John shook his head. "Here I am eating steak, and there're poor souls out there with nothing."

He looked at me. "Now Tziporah never would've done that. She'd have pushed them into the river. All of them. With the sole of her shoe."

He sipped his bourbon. "Enough of that," he said. "Let's change the subject." He put his hand across the smooth of my back the way Nigel used to. "Science," he said. "Black holes. That won't break your heart. Just keep you wondering." He noticed my salmon. "That looks good."

"Try some," I said.

"You sure? Thanks."

He stuck a piece of salmon with his fork and tasted it.

"That's really good! You know, I should start eating like that. Healthy."

By our second dinner together, I'd grown fond of his company, his openness, his warm heart.

M oments before the phone call, Pamela was light and happy, like a teenager before her birthday party. Her eyes, the seductive glint of crystal, the sparkle in her smile, the crinkling of her nose, flirtatious and bawdy, had vanished. There was now a dazed look, the sudden realization: life doesn't last forever.

She raised her champagne glass to drink, but it was empty. She looked at the glass as if to ask where it had gone. *How could it be empty? I'd just had it to my lips moments ago.*

I reached for the champagne bottle to refill her glass, but only a little came out. I motioned to the waiter.

She looked at me. "Mother wasn't joking. It really happened." She sat back in her chair as if gravity had pulled her back suddenly. She exhaled. "You don't think it can happen—not to you—not in your own family."

The waiter arrived with another bottle of champagne. He placed a fresh glass in front of Pamela and filled it. She stared at the bubbles.

"Well," she said, looking up at me, "am I acting strange? I feel strange." She finished nearly the whole glass of champagne in a single swallow.

"What did your mother say? It *was* her, right?"

"She sounded…" She fanned her face with her open hand. "It's like something out of a movie…" She finished the champagne left in her glass, and I refilled it.

"How did she sound?" I asked. "Your mother? Not herself?"

"No…it's hard to say."

I remembered the afternoon I'd been released from prison: Tziporah waiting in the limousine; her tone, the pleasure of controlled irony.

I asked Pamela, "Were the police there? With your mother?"

She shook her head. "No…She said something odd."

"Odd? How so?"

"I asked if they knew who did it. And she said yes, but the police wouldn't be involved. Said she'd handle it herself."

I wanted to ask more questions. I wanted some indication of Tziporah's intentions. Would she simply have Mohammed Algenib eliminate me? He was here. But that would be too simple. Where would the satisfaction be in that?

I ordered another bottle of champagne, and when the waiter arrived with it, I asked for vodka on ice. A double. Neither of us had finished our dinner. We were drinking on empty stomachs.

"I'm starting to feel the champagne." Pamela gazed out the window at the lights against the skyline. The moon was crescent. "It's so pretty…" She pushed her chair away from the table, started to her feet, and lost her balance. "Oops…"

I stood to help her, taking her arm.

"Take me to my room," she said.

She stared at me for a moment. I could see she was drunk. She took my arm to steady herself, and after several steps, she seemed more in control. I asked the waiter to charge everything to my suite and to add more than a little for himself. He bowed.

The elevator was a clear tube. The atrium lounge, far below, was just visible as we descended to the nineteenth floor. Pamela stood with her head resting on my shoulder. The light, airy scent of her perfume had faded to mix with her own scent. It wasn't as delicate but was stronger, sensual in a demanding way. The doors opened.

She handed me her handbag and said the keycard was somewhere in there. I looked through her bag for the card; I felt her lips touch my neck; she bit me, softly.

Once inside, and still in the foyer, she said, "You have to help me."

I helped her to the bedroom and switched on the nightlight. She sat on the edge of the bed and then lay back.

"Undress me," she said.

"Pamela, you've had too much to drink."

I removed her shoes and reached for a blanket to cover her. She took my hand and wouldn't let go.

"No," she said. "You have to stay."

I tried to leave, but she squeezed my hand.

"No," she said. "Please…"

With her other hand, she reached under her dress, raised her weight to one side, and pulled off her panties. "Lick me."

"What?"

"Lick me," she said again. "It's OK. I use perfume there… please."

<hr />

My clothes were on the floor. Pamela was asleep, lying on her stomach. I covered her with a cotton blanket. She moved, freeing her long, beautiful leg. I collected my things from the floor and stepped quietly from the room.

In the foyer I slipped on my underwear, my clothes, and then my shoes. I reached into my blazer pocket for my keycard. It wasn't there. I searched in the inside pocket. I found it.

I took the stairs down to the eighteenth floor. It was after 1:00 a.m. The fluorescent lights in the stairwell were harsh against my eyes. I was squinting when I stepped into the hall and started toward my suite.

I inserted the keycard in my door, when I was suddenly startled from behind.

"Did you enjoy yourself?"

I turned.

It was Mohammed Algenib. He continued to his room, stopped at the door, and then looked back at me.

At this point I knew very little about Mohammed Algenib. His history came later, pieced together through e-mails and stories retold among servants.

He was fourteen years old when he and his sixteen-year-old brother, Hanif, started working for Samira Khashi. They'd been orphaned years earlier through a tribal dispute that had claimed the lives of both parents in the deserts north of Medina. It's believed there was an uncle, a mentor of sorts, who'd been slain only weeks before the boys stole away from the remainder of the tribe to make their way across the desert to Egypt. The uncle was thought to have had indecent relations with another man, a vagabond of a warring tribe. The boys fled after viewing his execution.

Mohammed and Hanif went to work for Samira Khashi while she was married to the brother of Hussein bin Ali. Another servant had recommended them. "Upon all that is holy," it was claimed, "they are good Muslim boys."

At their age, well into puberty, they had suspected or already had given in to their sexual attractions. Both Mohammed and

Hanif possessed this gene. But Mohammed was far more discreet regarding the company he chose.

At the time Tziporah came into the family of Hussein bin Ali, Hanif was discovered in bed with a man, both of them naked. Hanif was dragged to an outlying area of the desert and beheaded with an Arabian sword. Mohammed was forced to watch.

Tziporah was furious.

Samira said it was a righteous outcome. "Such behavior is against God's law!" She was just inches from Tziporah's face.

Tziporah said it was no one's business—and *certainly* not God's—who one sleeps with!

Their hatred for each other had surfaced early.

Mohammed Algenib became increasingly loyal to Tziporah.

A year or so later, after Samira's death, a young man with whom Mohammed had fallen in love, Badi al Zaman, was arrested for "unholy acts" and sentenced to death. Publically Tziporah held her tongue, but she and Meyer negotiated with currency for the young man's release and sent him to New York, where he was soon employed through Meyer's connections.

While living in London, in faithful service to Meyer and Tziporah, Mohammed Algenib traveled to New York to visit an old friend he hadn't seen for nearly ten years. His friend was at the beginning stages of AIDS. The illness had started with an eye infection, prolonged fatigue, and then pneumonia.

Mohammed remained in New York for nearly a month after his friend's death to settle and dispose of the personal property among Badi al Zaman's closest friends in the city.

A year after Mohammed Algenib returned to London, and his service to Tziporah, he was tested positive for the HIV virus. He told Tziporah of the results and expected to leave her service. But she refused his offer to leave, and he continued on.

Mohammed Algenib then promised upon his soul that his very life belonged to Tziporah.

I didn't see Pamela the next day. She knocked several times on my door, but I didn't answer, and she didn't have my mobile number. The landline rang, off and on, all day, but I didn't answer that either. I felt lethargic—deeply melancholic. I didn't leave my suite until much later, after dark.

I ate a sandwich of sprouts and tofu I'd left on the counter the day before, and there was a bottle of wine in the refrigerator. I spent the afternoon lying on the sofa, staring out at the bay and the ocean in the distance. I fell asleep, awoke, took a carisoprodol, drank another glass of wine, and fell asleep again.

I shoveled snow from the roof in Philadelphia. Adrienne was zipped up in winter clothes. She carried Graham piggyback through the snow. They were laughing, fell into a snowdrift...I waited for them to reappear...but the snow started to melt. They were gone.

It was dark when I awoke. The moon had risen over the South China Sea. I felt a deep sense of isolation—a language I didn't understand, and the physical appearance of the people were alien to me. I had to disappear, but how? Facial recognition, bank transactions…Tziporah would find me. Giving up seemed easier.

The more dormant I remained, the more depressed I became. I had to move about, force oxygen through my system.

I didn't have a bathing suit, but my briefs were bright red with black stripes. Who could tell? I pulled khaki shorts on over my underwear, draped a bath towel around my neck, finished the last glass of wine on my way out the door, and entered the elevator.

The elevator went all the way to the roof. The doors opened to the pool area. The underwater lights gave a look of shimmering turquoise to the water. I dropped my towel on a lounge chair. The night air was warm and humid, like the touch of a moist hand.

There were few people at the pool. I lay back on the lounge chair. A waiter in a white jacket asked whether I wished to order anything.

"Champagne, thank you. Please bring the bottle."

I finished the first glass of champagne and remembered the two strawberries the young waitress, Layonna, had served with the croissant. As I opened my eyes from the memory of her, there she was, on the diving board, her beautiful legs stepping forward with precision as she entered into her dive, leaving the board, noise-lessly, her arms outstretched from her sides, her back arched as she entered the water without a splash.

I watched her broken image swim underwater to the edge of the pool. She surfaced.

"You are awake," she said. She raised herself out of the pool and sat on the edge, her legs still in the water. "I walked past you."

"Yes…I'm awake. You dive beautifully."

"The water is nice. You wish to come in?"

I joined her at the edge of the pool, my legs over the edge, and then dropped into the water. I swam underwater to the center of the pool with my eyes open. As I turned to surface, Layonna was in front of me.

"You surprised me," I said, breaking the surface.

I swam on my side, facing Layonna. Her sidestroke was smooth and elegant.

"Where did you learn to dive? It was beautiful to watch."

"I grew up on the water," she said.

We were holding the edge of the pool, facing each other.

"We are called sea gypsies," she continued. "This is not a compliment. But we are proud to be of the sea."

"You swim like a mermaid."

She laughed. "This is half fish, no?"

"I never thought of it that way. To me it's just a beautiful woman. But...I guess you could say 'half fish.'"

"Then I wish not to be a mermaid. Someone might eat me, no?" Her smile was so beautiful; I was star-struck.

"Join me for a glass of champagne?"

She hesitated.

"Please."

"I should not visit with guests. It is forbidden."

"Tell them I insisted, threatened to sue—"

"This is a joke, no?"

"Yes...of course. I was being—"

She started to laugh. "I understand," she said. "This was my joke."

This may have been the point at which I fell in love with her. I pulled myself out of the pool and then offered my hand to help her out of the water. She took my hand and raised herself up. She was as lissome as a feather in the breeze. I handed her my towel, and before I had turned around, the waiter had set another towel on the arm of the lounge chair. He returned also with fresh glasses of champagne. Layonna pushed a chair next to mine.

"What's a sea gypsy?" I asked. "It sounds romantic."

"It is what land people say of us." She sipped her champagne. "I was born on the sea. On my father's boat. My mother teaches me to read. My relatives...teach me Portuguese, Cantonese, Hindustani."

"Where did you learn English?"

"My cousin. His father is English."

"Your cousin?"

"He lives on land. His mother drown. Far at sea. He now lives with his boyfriend, and they teach me English."

"How long have you studied English?"

"Five years now. My father doesn't approve."

"Of English or your cousin?"

"Both." Layonna laughed. "This is hard for the old world to accept. But the *universe* makes us. We do not make ourselves."

She explained that she now lived on land and that this too upset her father. "I wish to learn new things," she said. "You are new, but you have been here many times."

"Many times?"

She placed her hand on my chest. "You…inside. The universe doesn't waste but uses many times what we're made of. You've been here before. I feel it."

"I love your company," I said. "It's refreshing—peaceful."

"Then we must spend time together."

She sipped her champagne and then said to me, "You are in underwear, no?"

Her smile was warm, but her charm came from somewhere much deeper. I searched for the right word, but it was unobtainable, elusive, a thought I couldn't form.

I asked whether she might meet me the next day; she said tomorrow was her day off, and she would find it a pleasure to spend time with me.

"A pleasure…" I heard this again and again in my thoughts as I lay in bed that night. A pleasure.

I wanted to avoid Pamela the next day. I had to avoid her. I never should have let that night with her happen. But as an excuse, I told myself I needed to know what Tziporah was up to. Her intentions might be revealed through Pamela. By now Tziporah knew I had been to bed with her daughter. Algenib would have seen to that.

I met Layonna the next morning outside the hotel. We had breakfast at a small restaurant nearly hidden from view by small trees and palm shrubs along a tiny street. Inside, dragonfly plants with long trailing white blossoms and philodendrons hung in windows. The owner was European, his wife Asian. He spoke French with an accent I hadn't heard since Paris. His wife bowed in a slight gesture and smiled. Layonna gave our order in Cantonese.

We were served scrambled eggs, French style, loose and creamy rich with butter. The coffee too was European. I sprinkled salt from the palm of my hand over my eggs the way I'd seen John Savensworth do.

"I wish to show you something," Layonna said. "Something special." The sound of her voice was feminine, pleasing to hear. "Where I grew up. You wish to see?"

"Yes. Where is it?"

"I will show you."

I rented a small car, using a Pennsylvania driver's license, seven years expired, and with a last name that didn't match my new passport. The rental agent appeared leery. Speaking for me, Layonna answered his questions in Cantonese, although the agent spoke English. She answered with an aplomb that seemed to indicate the agent's skepticism was misplaced. He finished the paperwork, looking up at me now and then. In the end he handed me the keys as though he were still unconvinced.

We drove north for nearly an hour toward the mouth of the Pearl River, and the road then turned east. Layonna said to continue this way. It was hard to believe a part of the world so densely populated could appear so remote and inaccessible.

"Who are you?" she asked. "You have many names."

"That will take some explaining."

"Maybe in your underwear," she said with a smile, "in the pool, you will tell me."

"I don't have a bathing suit. The underwear was a simple solution."

"You don't respect law, do you?"

"The law? The law is superfluous."

"Super…?"

"It means unnecessary."

She thought for a moment. "I like this word."

We followed a dirt road along an estuary. The banks were thick with candlenut and pine trees, and around a bend, the inlet widened and formed another river. Through the clearing along the riverbank, there were several boats, houseboats, tied to a dock made of logs and thick branches of bamboo tied together.

The houseboat Layonna pointed out as her parents' home had two bamboo masts and a roof, with bamboo awnings over the windows. An older woman, Asian, brown from the sun, sat at a small table, sewing something. As we approached she stood and smiled at Layonna. They exchanged words, sentences, in Cantonese, and then Layonna turned and introduced me and said this was her mother.

He mother welcomed me and motioned with her hand for me to take a seat. I stepped aboard.

Layonna and her mother spoke, and Layonna turned to me and asked if I wished to have tea. I looked to her mother; she nodded and smiled.

"Yes," I said. "Thank you."

Layonna said something to her mother, and her mother then went inside. A moment later a man appeared from inside the boat. He looked to be in his late fifties, Indian in appearance, with a slight wave to his black hair. He wore a loose pullover cotton shirt with a V-neck opening. Layonna said something to him, and he looked at me for a moment and then came forward to offer his hand. His look was serious, almost stern, as though I were being inspected.

Her mother returned with tea and small white cups on a wicker tray and set it on the sewing table she had cleared of cloth, needles, and thread.

There was an awkward silence as the water lapped gently against the side of the boat, with the cry of a cockatoo in the trees and then another.

"This is where we come to make repairs," Layonna said. "And to rest from the government."

"The government?"

She said something in Cantonese to her father, and he answered her. She turned to me. "The government wish to make us disappear—sea gypsies. We are..." She turned to her father, spoke

140

to him, and he answered. She turned back to me. "Embarrassment. The government wish to look modern. They say this is good for everyone. The one person—"

"The individual," I said. "The individual means nothing to them."

"Yes." She explained this to her father. He nodded and said something in Cantonese but then switched to Portuguese.

"My father thinks you are wise," Layonna said. "He say without the individual you are the anthill. Not human."

I finished a second cup of tea while Layonna spoke casually with her mother, and then she turned to me. "My parents wish you to share a meal. Here, on our home."

"Yes," I said. "Of course."

She turned to her father with my answer. His smile was reserved but warm.

Layonna and her mother prepared our meal in a section of the boat under a window covered with a bamboo awning. The smoke seemed to waft out the open window on its own; I smelled ginger and cinnamon. Her father and I sat at the stern of the boat in comfortable silence.

The meal was whitefish and rice with a green vegetable mixed with the rice. This was where the ginger and cinnamon added a unique flavor. I sipped my hot tea and smiled toward Layonna's mother. She returned my smile. Her father appeared stoic, unmoved by the sudden cry of a cockatoo in the trees.

When I later returned to the hotel, I found Pamela sitting on the floor outside my door, exasperated.

"Where have you been?"

I removed my keycard and inserted it in the lock. She followed me in.

"It's almost dark," she said, standing at the window, a wall of glass, overlooking the harbor. She turned. "You've been avoiding me. For two days now." She came forward. "Did I do something wrong?" She played with the button on my shirt. "What's that smell?"

"Smell?"

"Where've you been?"

"Nowhere. I don't know…"

"Nowhere? For two days?"

I didn't answer.

"Nicky, what's wrong? Something bothering you?"

"I've asked you not to call me Nicky. Please."

She shrugged as if what I'd said meant little to her, but my insistence had hurt her feelings. She walked toward the kitchenette and opened the refrigerator door.

"It's empty!" She opened the freezer door. "Vodka. That's it? What do you eat?"

Jesus. I just wanted her to go.

"You'll never guess," she said. She closed the refrigerator door and stepped closer to me. "Not in a million years."

"What?"

"My mother's coming. To Hong Kong."

My stomach sank.

"My God," Pamela said. "Don't look so pale. *You* don't have to put up with her. I do."

"Why?"

"Why do I have to put up with her? Don't be silly."

"No. Why is she coming? *Here.*"

"She's still upset. About Uncle Meyer. I still can't believe it."

"When…when is she coming?"

"Look at you. You'd think it was *your* mother."

She smoothed my collar around my neck and slid her hands down my chest. "What's that smell? Ginger?"

"When does she get here?"

"My mother? Not for a month or so." She sniffed my shirt. "She has things to do in London first. You smell like smoke."

I poured some vodka from the freezer. I filled a wineglass and took a drink.

Pamela started unbuttoning my shirt. "I'll take you in the shower," she said, crinkling her nose. "I'll make you smell good."

Tziporah, I thought. I knew I'd have to face her. *But I can leave… just disappear? I have money.*

Pamela undid my belt, placed her thumb and forefinger inside the waistband of my underwear and slid them down. She removed her clothes, took me by the hand, and led me into the shower.

During our time together in Paris, I'd once met John Savensworth in a seldom-used park. It was late afternoon. A few early leaves had fallen from the trees to checker the grass. A woman on a bicycle passed an old man on a bench as pigeons strutted in small circles in front of him. He shelled peanuts and tossed them to the pigeons. The passing bicycle caused several pigeons take flight.

I was walking to clear my head, when I ran into Savensworth. He was by himself. He had a rolled-up newspaper under his arm and a bag of peanuts in one hand. He threw a handful of peanuts toward the base of a tree to a squirrel that chirped and flicked its tail as though it were expecting to be fed.

"I once saw a photograph of this park," he said. "In black and white. It was taken after the war. A boy sat on a bench, over there, reading a newspaper. He was maybe ten or eleven. He looked so intent. *What's he reading?* I wondered as I stared at the picture. *What's he thinking?* The city had just been liberated. What had he seen—heard—during the occupation? How quickly was he forced to grow up?"

John took a few more peanuts from the bag and tossed them to another squirrel that had joined the first one. Both were flicking their tails.

"How many murders do you think happened—private murders," he asked, "during the occupation? There was no 'rule of law.' Not really. The country had been invaded. The powerful devoured the weak."

We had walked toward a weathered bench and sat down.

"I nearly committed a murder," he said. "My heart was certainly in it. All that was missing was opportunity."

I looked at him.

He nodded as if to reaffirm his confession.

"I considered drowning him. In the river. I'd even planned it out," he said. "I was living in Philadelphia at the time. Not that long ago. I was walking along the banks of the Schuylkill. A group of colored boys, a pack of five or six, started throwing stones at me. They were cursing and calling me 'whitey, cracker.' The names didn't mean anything to me. It was the stones. I got pelted several times. At first I was stunned—I couldn't figure out what was happening. Then I grabbed a handful of stones and started throwing at them. I hit one, and the whole pack took off. As they ran off, I called after them, 'Nigger bastards!' Just then a white kid, tall, blondish boy, maybe in his twenties, passed me on a bike. He stopped about twenty feet in front of me and yelled back, 'Racist Nazi!' Then he rode toward me and circled me on his bike. 'Nazi racist, Nazi racist!' he shouted in my face."

John sat back and crossed his legs. He looked inside the bag of peanuts, stuck his hand in but didn't remove it. "I don't think I've ever been so enraged as I was at that moment. Somehow that kid on the bike, in my eyes, had ceased to be human. I felt attacked. Again. For what?"

John got to his feet. "Would you care for coffee? There's a café over there. We can sit outside."

I said it sounded fine, and we cut across the park toward the street. "But that wasn't the end of him," John said as we walked. "He showed up every time I walked along the river. He called after me—yelled it out—'Racist! Nazi!' In front of people. Strangers. A man might think he's free of public opinion—above it—but we're not."

He looked at me. "This guy saw himself as the law *and* executioner. And in doing so, he took away my freedom. Who gave him the right? The power?"

The café had a brown awning with white piping along edges. There were several wrought-iron tables and chairs with cushions out front. We stepped onto the sidewalk.

"We have to get the coffee ourselves," John said.

Inside, the café smelled of yeast and pastries, fresh from the oven. We got two coffees, both black, in white cups, and returned to the tables out front.

"But you never did it?" I said. "You never went after him?"

"No. But the intent was there. Without any thought of right or wrong. I wanted to do it. Not just to shut him up. I saw in him a person capable of torture. At first it starts with small animals, but then it graduates…"

He looked across the street at the park.

"What do you think it was like during the occupation? This city? What was the stronger force—the Germans or public opinion?"

He clasped his hand on my shoulder and then ran it along the smooth of my back.

"Let's change the subject," he said in a more jovial tone. "Would you like more coffee? I would."

But my inner thoughts, my mood, didn't change. What would I do to free myself of another person's control, manipulation?

Murder seemed acceptable.

It was.

Passing clouds first appeared in front of the moon, and then the moon clouded over to just a haze and then disappeared. The lighted yachts out on the harbor had become less visible in the thick, humid air.

I opened the freezer door, poured vodka into a wineglass, and drank half. I found a bath towel in the hall closet, draped it around my neck, but then hesitated. Did I want another drink?

No. You're drinking too much.

I took the elevator up to the roof. As the doors opened to the shimmering turquoise of the pool, it started to rain. An awning of green-and-white stripes opened automatically from the elevator side of the building and stretched over the length of the pool. There was a light mist rising from the heated water, and my mermaid appeared. She surfaced, her head slightly back, her black hair slicked, her teeth sparkling.

"Hello, my Nicholas."

There were tears in my heart at the sound of "My Nicholas."

"Hello."

"I have a surprise for you." Layonna's smile was so pure, her eyes slightly crinkled at the corners. She raised herself out of the pool, water flowing from her figure, smiling as she came forward.

"I have made for you something."

She removed a cover from a platter on the end table next to our lounge chairs. She held the platter up. "You must taste."

They were tiny cake-like squares no more than an inch. I put one in my mouth.

"Oh my God, it's wonderful! What are they?"

"There is much cheese," she said, patting her stomach. "Not good for this. And apple brandy and rice. So you like my treat?"

"They're delicious."

"Come," she said, taking me by the hand. At the edge of the pool, she said, "Jump with me."

We splashed into the water together. I swam to the bottom of the pool and turned, and Layonna faced me, her eyes open, smiling, tiny bubbles escaping from her nose. As I started for the surface, she wrapped her elegant legs around my waist, and we surfaced together.

The water was still in my eyes when I said, "Dive for me. I want to watch."

"I will dive for you," she said and swam for the ladder at the deep end of the pool.

I pulled myself up and onto the edge of the pool, my legs still in the water.

Layonna stepped onto the diving board, stood perfectly straight for a moment, and then, with precision steps, she started toward the end of the board; her left knee rose as she went up and then came down soundlessly on the end of the board. The momentum sent her straight up, her head tilted back, and then into a reverse summersault to enter the water like an arrow.

I watched her broken image swim underwater as she came toward the edge of pool and grabbed my ankles.

She surfaced, smiling. "Was this good to watch?"

"It was beautiful." I reached forward to take her face in my hands. At that moment I would have given my life for her.

⊷ ⊷

When Layonna got her driver's license, she felt a sense of accomplishment and transition. The transition led her further away from the world of the sea and into a modern, urbanized world. She was a mermaid leaving her element.

I wanted to buy her a car, but she had seen an electric motor scooter on a showroom floor in Kowloon.

"I like this," she said. "It doesn't smell of fumes. And makes only quiet noise."

The scooter was red, with a black seat for two, and had a basket in front. It had a range of more than a hundred kilometers with a speed of sixty kilometers an hour. Layonna said she could manage the price with thriftiness, but I asked if she would please allow me to pay for it. She didn't answer but looked at me. While her hand was at her side, I slipped my debit card between her fingers. She glanced up at me.

"Please…" I said in a gentle tone.

She nodded.

In another part of the world, the sales agent might have asked for some form of identification to match the name on the debit card. But the card had been issued through the Construction Bank of China, and this wasn't some other part of the world. The papers were signed, and a plate was attached to the back of the scooter. When Layonna turned the ignition key, the engine was so quiet I didn't think it was running.

"Come," she said, "you are my first ride with me." She patted the backseat with her hand.

An electric motor scooter of all things. I fell in love with it. The speed was remarkable, and it was so quiet. Layonna seemed hesitant at first to gather speed, but within minutes her courage grew with her skill. In less than twenty minutes, we were weaving through traffic, passing cars, and soon arrived in the area of the small restaurant where we'd had breakfast a few weeks earlier. She turned onto the same street of small trees and palm shrubs. The street narrowed and came to an end, a tiny cul-de-sac, with only one building remaining.

Layonna stopped in front of an iron gate ornamented with the profile of a black swan. I held the motor scooter between my out-stretched legs, while she entered a security code. The gate opened to a narrow alleyway, and she drove to the end. She stopped the motor scooter, set the kickstand in place, and with an outstretched hand said, "This is my place to live."

The outside door was painted red, and on each side of it were potted plants. On the front of the door, there were Chinese characters in gold: 水少女.

"What's this?" I asked. "Numbers?"

"No. My cousin puts this here. *Water Maiden.* This is his building. He lives here with his boyfriend."

She unlocked the door, and we went inside. The room was tiny but uncluttered. The bathroom was no bigger than a closet, with a stool and a shower. There was a kitchen countertop of blue stone with white grout, a two-burner stove, and a toaster oven. The floor was carpeted, and under the window was a futon with drawers at the bottom. White-grass plants hung in the window. Along the windowsill were books, many of which were Mandarin poetry, translated into English and Cantonese.

"This is my home," she said.

Layonna prepared egg-drop soup, whitefish, and rice, served with green tea. We ate cross-legged on the floor at a small wooden table. We later pulled out the futon and looked up through the window as the day slowly faded and dusk tinted the sky pink before it turned a deep velvety-blue.

When I awoke, the sky was filled with stars. I looked for familiar stars, constellations, but my view was limited from where I lay. The stars looked foreign. Layonna lay on her side, facing me. Her breathing was peaceful. She looked so beautiful sleeping, so innocent, yet not.

⊷ ⊶

Days later, as I descended from the eighteenth floor, through the glass atrium of the hotel, I saw Pamela talking to Layonna in the lobby. By the time the elevator arrived on the first floor, Layonna was gone. Pamela saw me. It seemed she had been on her way out, but she now came toward me with a huge smile.

"How ya doin', handsome?" With a playful Texas tone and gesture, she poked me in the side. "Were ya lookin' fer me?"

"Actually, I was…" I glanced toward the lounge; Layonna was gone from sight. "…on my way out."

"Why? What are you up to? Want company?"

Her childlike manner was disarming, somehow refreshing.

"Well, I was going to pick up my tuxedo."

"*Oh*," she said, "that's right! You promised me a formal dinner."

"A what?"

"I know just the place. Macau. Mother knows this sheik who has a boat. He parties on it. It's like a restaurant or something."

"Your mother?"

"She gets here next week."

Outside the hotel, Pamela asked the doorman to call us a cab.

"When?" I asked.

"When what?"

"Your mother—when is she supposed to be here?"

"Oh God! Won't that be fun?" She rolled her eyes.

The doorman opened the cab door for us.

"Do you know that Asian girl?" she asked. "Who works in the lounge? I was talking to her. She's pretty special—really different. You know…she reminds me of something like a mermaid. Pretty odd, isn't it? A mermaid. Good lord. But she's really sweet."

I gave the driver the tailor's address.

England had denied Meyer's citizenship request, John once explained; cash-for-questions was a fog that never had cleared. That's when Meyer bought the castle in Scotland. John had been invited several times to spend long weekends at the castle during the winter months. Tziporah no longer made excuses as to why she couldn't (wouldn't) sleep in John's bed. She assigned him his own bedroom and a chambermaid to entertain him. Whereas another man might not have endured the oblique insult, John was so consumed with the ideas of science that it insulated him from direct injury. And he was grateful for the time with his daughter.

After England's second denial of citizenship, Meyer then claimed to be of Egyptian blood, insisting his line went all the way back to antiquity.

"That's when I first noticed odd behaviors," John said. "He once had an article printed, like you'd find in encyclopedias. The piece was all about him. He had the encyclopedia reprinted and the pages inserted. I think he wanted Pamela to see it. To impress her, maybe. But she was too young to understand. So what was the point?"

John asked whether I wanted a croissant. We were having coffee at Starbucks in Belgravia, London. It was only days before I was supposed to have killed him. The weather was overcast, damp, with a cold chill that I found hard to endure.

"Yes, thank you."

"Extra butter? I like the butter as thick as soup on a day like today."

I smiled and said, "Yes. Extra butter."

He returned with two croissants on a white plate. The croissants were cut lengthwise but not all the way through, and the butter lay in the middle, a yellowy liquid. John picked up his croissant, and as he bit into it, the butter dripped from it, and he held his hand under it to catch the runny butter.

"Oh shit," he said, smiling, and then licked the butter from his palm. "I'm not always this messy. Honest."

I cut the croissant into sections on my plate and tried to avoid the mess.

"Meyer was almost a child himself," John said. "In that he couldn't see there was no competition for Pamela. She loved him. But the idea of sharing her was painful for him. No, impossible. It was all or nothing. Why is that?"

Silence followed.

"Pamela was playing outside once," he continued. "We were both there, Meyer and me. We watched her play—without a word between us—watching, each in our own way, when she fell. She was on a path of crushed cinders. She couldn't have been any more than seven years old. She started to cry, and when she stood up, she saw blood on her hands and cried louder. Well, she ran toward us. Meyer held out his arms to take her and give her comfort, but she ran to me instead. I saw from the corner of my eye how that hurt him. I said, 'Honey, show Uncle Meyer. He'll help make it better.' But she ignored him and clung to me, her arms around my neck."

As I heard the story, my heart went out to Meyer. But then I remembered our last luncheon together in Paris and Meyer's instructions to me.

"Later that day," John said, "I saw Meyer out back in the garden, with a shotgun. He was shooting birds out of the trees. Innocent birds. There must have been a dozen on the ground. Why? What was the sense to it?"

I looked down and saw I had dripped butter on my hands.

I wiped them clean.

The thought of facing Tziporah filled me with dread, a hollow weight over my heart. No matter how it ended between us, it wouldn't end well. I wanted to disappear. Australia came to mind: Perth, Australia. The physical remoteness was almost dreamlike, a fantasy, a fictional escape.

I could take Layonna with me, but then I'd have to explain my past to her, my reason for running. Money was no longer an obstacle, yet without Layonna I had nothing, and to take her with me would turn her into a fugitive.

"You are sad, my Nicholas. What is this word you say?" She looked at me with the face of a student. "Melody...?"

"Melancholy?"

"Yes," she said, now smiling. "This word is like music, no? I find it in the dictionary. I hear you say this word. I like the meaning. It is like sad music to hear."

"Have you ever been to Australia?"

"No. This is my home. The sea. Hong Kong. But not the sea so much," she added. "I am changing."

"Layonna, I'm not who you think I am."

"I know this," she said. "Inside every man, there are many people. Many deeds."

She took me by the hand to tug me forward.

"Come," she said. "We will go into dark Hong Kong. Where the old ways still live."

"Tourist traps?"

"No. I show you."

We rode Layonna's motor scooter through the streets of Kowloon. I was sitting behind her. Her hair in the night air, as we rode through the city streets, smelled of spice and her skin of the sea and coconut. Strands of her hair blew into my mouth. I held them between my lips. She reached her hand back to squeeze my leg.

At first the streets were new and modern, paved, with digital-advertising billboards that followed you with human eyes as though stalking you—and then the streets gradually became less modern, older, the air less industrialized but more human in their scent of labor, happiness, pleasure, lust, the need to live.

The roads were now crowded with people on foot. Layonna pulled into an alley next to an Indian restaurant. She said the restaurant belonged to a relative; it was safe to leave the motor scooter there. But still she locked it through the front wheel and the steering column.

Before we left the alley, a man emerged from the rear door of the kitchen. He had wavy black hair, shiny in the visible light through the kitchen door. The front of his white apron was stained with blood. He smiled and said something to Layonna, but it wasn't in Cantonese. She responded in a language that sounded melodic. They smiled at each other, but his glance toward me was indifferent, if not cold.

It was night but difficult to know the time. The people in the streets had an air of permanence, history without time. Cloth awnings extended from the fronts of the shops to cover nearly all the street, leaving only an alleyway of night sky above. Layonna led me by the hand. I heard firecrackers, saw the smoke rising, and smelled the sulfur. She led me into an open shop. Roasted ducks, cherry red, hung on strings, and metal tubs contained living creatures from the sea, waiting to be eaten. I became uncomfortable. Squeamish. I saw what looked like alcohol for sale by the glass. Vodka and rum. I slowed down, and Layonna looked at me. She saw what I was doing and waited. I pointed to a bottle of vodka, and Layonna told the man what I wanted. They spoke for a moment in Cantonese, as if discussing price.

I asked for a second glass. I drank it without pause.

I pulled a number of crushed bills from my pocket, and Layonna picked several of them from my hand and paid for the drinks. She and the man exchanged a few words, and we moved on.

We came to a much larger area in the street, an open bazaar. The stalls were filled with rolls of cloth, jewelry, cutlery, cheap handheld devices, electronics. The air was close with the sickly sweet smell of spices. A dozen people or so were gathered around a stand with sides that formed a barrier a foot high around a table. Within the perimeter of the tabletop stand, there was a snake, maybe seven feet long, brownish gray. Scattered around the snake were bills, paper money. The men argued back and forth as though wagers were being made.

"You see this?" Layonna said. "This is death. The black mamba. These men bet who can take the money."

The venom of the black mamba is the deadliest known. Death follows within minutes of the bite. The nervous system is paralyzed, and it's one of the fastest snakes on the planet.

I noticed that I'd become of more interest than the snake. Several of the men were looking at me and talking among themselves. One laughed and then another.

"What's this?" I asked Layonna.

"They think white man should try."

I laughed. "I don't think so."

A man with a brownish complexion said something to the others, and they laughed, all turning toward me.

"What was that about?"

"Nothing," Layonna said. "We must go."

The man with the brownish complexion said in English, "You must be coward." Then he turned to the others and spoke in Cantonese. They all looked at me as though the insult had been translated.

"Come," Layonna said. "We must go." She tugged at my arm.

"Wait. Who is this guy?" I said, looking at the man.

"He speaks with Vietnam sound."

"His accent? Vietnamese?"

"Come," she said.

"No, goddamn it." I stepped toward the table and the black mamba while staring at the Vietnamese man. Silence followed.

I looked down at the snake. Its head and nearly two feet of its body were raised in a striking position. The slightest movement of my hand made the snake move in that direction. I reached forward with both arms, extended to the side, out of the snake's striking distance. I made a sudden movement with my left hand, and the snake turned its head toward the movement. At that moment I snapped it up with my right hand, at the neck, just below the head. The snake curled itself around my forearm and biceps in vain effort. Stunned silence descended upon the crowd. I turned and faced them with the helpless snake in my grip.

With my left hand, I gathered all the bills from the table, turned toward the Vietnamese man, and pushed the money into his shirt pocket as I held the openmouthed black mamba in front of him. Holding the snake tightly by the neck, I pulled it from my arm and then dropped it onto the enclosed table. There were a few words, a few whispers behind me, but I didn't turn around.

Only a few yards from the bazaar, as I stopped for another drink, did I feel my heart pounding. *Jesus Christ*, I thought. *What did I just do?* Layonna looked at me in silence. I glanced back at the snake table. That's when I saw him. Mohammed Algenib. He was talking to the snake handler.

How did he get here? Did he follow us? How...?

Mohammed and the snake handler seemed to have come to an agreement, as Mohammed handed the snake handler a roll of bills the color of Hong Kong currency. The snake handler used a hooked stick to take the snake from the enclosed table and drop it into a cloth bag. He handed it to Mohammed. I watched a moment longer before I realized...he had bought the goddamn snake.

S heik Mohammed bin Rashid Al Zayed sailed his yacht under the flag of Oman and claimed Muscat as his home port. He anchored the five-hundred-foot yacht within sight of Macau. He came to Macau for the gambling, but he didn't sail there. He flew from Qatar to Macau International Airport, and from there he was taken by private launch to his yacht. Nights of unsuccessful gambling in Macau satisfied his self-image of stealthy courage at the tables and offered amusement to those who pitied him while they watched. Tziporah used him as one who would guide a blind man through a room of furniture.

The main deck of his yacht—under a night full of stars with a sea so calm the candles never flickered—was the setting for my formal dinner with Pamela. A dinner invitation I'd never offered or had imagined would happen. But the dinner hadn't come about through an artful ploy by Pamela. She was as artless as her father.

We were taken from the hotel in a Mercedes with a driver in chauffer's attire. I had explained to Layonna that was I attending a black-tie affair that night and that I was escorting a young English lady. I told her that it was part of a background, my personal history that I had yet to reveal and that I was hesitant for her to know me fully. She said she was sad not to go—*melancholy* is the word she used—"because such a word is mystical, yes?"

The chauffeured Mercedes dropped us at a private pier, and from there we were taken by launch out to the yacht, a mile or so from Macau. The sheik welcomed us aboard. He wore a tuxedo with a red vest; his hair and beard were dyed black against his aging, sallow skin. We had met before—the sheik and I—that night in Paris when Tziporah had introduced the sheik to John and me and then excused herself from our dinner engagement.

The sheik now offered his hand and welcomed us aboard his yacht. He feigned never having seen me before. He played it well. He turned to a fawning manner with Pamela and said how special her mother was to him, and even more so now, he added, as he glanced back at me, "in her hour of grief."

"Please, you are my guests." He held his hand toward our table. "Come…"

He held Pamela's chair for her and slid it under her. I seated myself.

There were several other tables on deck with guests seated at them. The entire deck had the feel of a stage setting, and the other guests were merely props. Somewhere above the city of Macau, fireworks lit up the night sky.

"Oh, look," Pamela said. "How pretty!"

"The view from the bow," the sheik said to me, "is very special. You must see it before you go."

I glanced toward the bow and then glanced at it a second time, while he continued to watch me. Is that what Samira Khashi was told the day she disappeared into the Mediterranean? "You must see it before you go"?

The sheik left us, and champagne was brought to our table. Our waiter opened the bottle, filled our glasses, and placed the bottle in an ice bucket next to the table. I drank the first glass rather quickly, and before I could reach for the bottle, the waiter refilled my glass. I looked up at him. There was a slight condescension in his eyes, a kind of pity without sympathy. It irked me, his presumption, the judgment, his secret knowledge.

"You look so nice," Pamela said, "in your tux. You should wear it more often."

"If it were the 1920s, I'd wear it every evening for dinner."

"I love old black-and-white pictures," she said. "And the movies. Everything looked so special then."

"So what have you heard from your mother?"

"Oh, look!" she said.

A bowl of large strawberries and cheese was brought to our table and placed at the center.

"I love these," she said, taking a strawberry from the bowl. She pinched the green stem off and took a bite. "Delicious," she said and then put the rest of it in her mouth. "I could eat a ton of these."

She wiped her fingers on the edge of the tablecloth. By the time she'd finished the strawberries, the white cloth looked as though it were covered with lipstick prints.

"Just one more," she said and then took a drink of champagne. "My mother?" She took another strawberry and pinched off the stem. "God, I love these."

"Yes. When do you expect her?" I refilled my glass.

"Actually she should've been here by now." She reached for another strawberry. "Just one more..."

"What's holding her up?"

"Don't know. I really don't. Mohammed what's-his-name is avoiding me. So I can't ask him. Or it seems he is avoiding me. He wasn't always like that when I was a girl. He changed after New York; he was there almost a year. He's queer, you know. He does to other men what I do to you—when you let me."

"Pamela, I'm old enough to be your father."

"Don't ruin everything…Anyway, he's worked for my mother a long time, since before I was born. And there's some secret between them. I heard the servants talking about it. They spoke in Arabic, so I only got part of it."

"What secret?"

"Something to do with Uncle Meyer's dead wife…I still can't believe he's dead; it doesn't seem possible. Anyway, there was a fight between my mother and Samira. She came after her with a knife—"

"Who? Your mother? Samira?"

"No, Samira did. You didn't think my mother, did you? Although you've got to hear about the rat. You won't believe this. She killed it with her bare hands."

"Bare hands? A rat?"

"You've got to hear this…"

I wanted to take Layonna shopping, but she said she didn't want anything. She suggested a picnic instead.

"What to do with things you have but have no need for? A picnic is different—then I'm next to you. I smell you...Do you know how you smell to me? Like pine trees—a smell cold and clean but sometimes warm. I like this."

Layonna made sandwiches of tofu and cheese with crisp lettuce between the layers. She mixed yellow mustard and saffron to create a garnish and spread it over the cheese. I added a bottle of Riesling to the basket attached to the front of her motor scooter, and Layonna placed a blanket in the basket, along with our lunch. The blanket was red, decorated with gold dragons. She said the dragons were there to protect us. "We lie between them," she said, "and we are protected."

Layonna drove the motor scooter, and I rode behind her on the long seat. She took the curves at a greater speed as her skill and confidence grew. We leaned toward the side at an angle as she followed the winding roads up the hillsides and then down toward the ocean and then up again. We came to a grassy plateau, and she pulled off to the side of the road. Far below we saw the traffic following the curvy road, but the traffic, on the other side of the hill, went in a different direction, and we were alone with the view of the harbor and the islands farther out.

I was eager for the wine. I poured a glass and drank it down before I offered any to Layonna. I had become too dependent on the false feelings of alcohol, but I didn't listen to my own reasoning. Layonna saw my need for alcohol, but she didn't say anything; she didn't ask why, neither with her eyes nor between her words. Had there been something admonishing in her eyes, a silent scolding, I may have found courage enough to pull away from her to save myself, but courage would have forced me to lay out my story for her to judge. The thought of losing her was too painful.

The wineglasses were made of hard plastic and were as clear as glass. I filled one for her; bubbles rose to the surface of the wine. She sipped it while looking at me.

I lay back on the blanket. From the corner of my eye, I saw the head of a gold dragon, as though it were watching me.

"Layonna, I must tell you something…"

She touched my lips with her fingertips.

Why did I love her so deeply?

"You wish me to go with you?" she asked, looking down at me. "I will do this."

"Yes? Western Australia. Or Hawaii. Miami?"

She laid her head on my chest, her hair against my lips.

"Then we should have a boat, no?" I heard the smile in her voice, the pleasure of the ocean in her thoughts.

"Yes," I said, "and you will pick it out. Whatever kind you want."

"I can hear your heart," she said, her ear next to my chest.

"What does it say?"

She raised her head to look at me, her hair falling forward, as she pushed it back with one hand. "It says, 'Then we sail to Hong Kong—to visit my father, yes?'"

I laughed. "Yes, it does say that. It says we will become sailors of the seven seas."

"No," Layonna said. She rolled onto her back, her head on my stomach. "There is only one ocean. Not seven. And under this ocean lives a goddess. She rules all she can swim to—and more. She looks for a man-god to be her lover. When they make love, the ocean is rough and wavy on top. Foamy waves crash onto the beach. When they are finished, the ocean is calm—very still." She rolled onto her side to look at me. "This boat will be our home, no?"

"Yes. Anything you want."

"Then I will fish for us. I will dive into the water to bring us food. Fish that are white and some that are many colors. We will store rice onboard."

I could picture it: Layonna diving from the bow to swim beneath the surface, her lithe body descending like a wavy ribbon through the water, her fishing spear in hand, as she swam toward her prey.

She reached forward to kiss me on the lips and then laid her head back on my chest to gaze up at the sky.

Over her shoulder I saw a jetliner coming into Hong Kong airspace. It was low as it disappeared behind the clouds and then reappeared on final approach, descending toward the airport. Inbound, I thought, from somewhere in Europe or America.

Or London.

Before his horrific death on Hong Kong Island, Mohammed Algenib gave me a more complete story of what had happened years earlier between Tziporah and Samira Khashi on the bow of the yacht. He approached me in the hotel lobby and, in a cordial manner, asked me to join him in the bar. He wore a white silk shirt, tucked in at the waist, and a black leather belt with a silver buckle. He wore the shirt open at the collar by two buttons. His skin was olive, his eyes brown, and when he smiled, he was pleasant to look at.

When he first spoke to me in the lobby, I was startled. My impression of him, created through the earlier stories I'd heard, was sinister, unsettling, and now, as he held an open hand toward the bar in an invitation to join him, I was taken off guard. I paused longer than I should have, and in this pause, he must have realized his advantage. Unable to find a word in response, I followed the direction of his hand, indicating the seclusion of the bar, the intimate lighting.

Several people were sitting around the tiny, round tables, but Mohammed and I were the only two at the bar itself. The barman set cloth napkins in front of us, and while smiling, he asked for our orders. I asked for dry sherry, neat. Mohammed asked for ginger ale. He was on a medication that didn't tolerate alcohol well, he explained, and then smiled as if in apology—a very attractive smile against his complexion.

There was some small talk at first, cursory words, before the sherry on my empty stomach gave me the courage to ask, "What's the point of this? This meeting?"

"Tziporah will be here shortly." He had a slight English accent that I found pleasant to the ear. "And I wish you to know certain things before she arrives."

"Are you here to kill me?"

"No," he answered. "I haven't been given that order." Again the smile. "You are very pleasing to the eyes," he said, "actually...quite pretty. What a loss that would be."

"Are you making fun of me?"

"No," he said, and in his face and eyes, I realized his answer didn't ring true. It had a false tone, tart, condescendingly flirtatious. I drained my glass.

"I was there," he said.

"You were where?"

"On the bow. Many years ago," he said. "When Samira fell from the yacht. You have repeated this story. You have put it in writing to use against us. But it's not true. I was there. Tziporah defended herself against Samira."

"Defended?"

The barman was looking our way. I touched my empty glass with my finger, and he refilled it. Algenib didn't answer while the barman refilled my glass.

"Samira was jealous," he said as the barman stepped away. "She didn't like the closeness Tziporah had for Meyer. But Tziporah wasn't good at hiding her affections. She and Meyer took chances. Samira found them in a playful wrestling game. Meyer's hand was under Tziporah's skirt. They were giggling as they wrestled together. Samira then knew the truth."

"How do you know this?"

"I saw it. I knew what existed between them. They didn't hide it from me—and they knew of my *preferences*."

"So what did happen on the bow?"

"It was Samira's intention to eliminate her rival. She had a knife with her. She tried to kill Tziporah. I saw the struggle from the bridge. Before I could get there, the knife was in Samira's chest, and she fell from the boat. The blood drew sharks, and she was pulled under."

I didn't know what to say. It sounded real.

"And Tziporah had nothing to do with the death of Johnathan Allyson," he added. "She argued against it. Meyer ordered it."

"Did you carry it out?"

"Yes."

"I don't understand," I said. "Why would you tell me this?"

Over Algenib's shoulder I saw Pamela. She was in the lobby when she'd caught sight of us in the bar. She now came toward the bar. Her smile was pretty.

Algenib looked to see what had caught my attention. He looked back at me. "She's very taken with you," he said, "but your attention is drawn to someone else. What are you going to do?"

At that point Pamela arrived at my side. She looped her arm through mine and looked at Algenib. "You trying to steal him?" Her smile beamed. "Bet you can't…"

Exercise with a hangover is painful even to consider, let alone begin, but once you start, the oxygen flows through your brain, and your thoughts begin to clear, and the headache subsides. Within several minutes the headache is gone.

The treadmill faced the glass wall overlooking the harbor. I was in black running shorts and a white T-shirt with a gold dragon over the pocket. I had the treadmill speed set at five miles per hour; fifteen minutes elapsed and then thirty and then forty-five. Sweat dripped from my face, and my T-shirt was soaked.

I saw Pamela's reflection in the glass wall as she came up behind me. Her cheerfulness was missing; her expression was serious and timid as she approached. Maybe Tziporah was here, and Pamela had gotten a call from her? But the look on her face was different from that. Tziporah wasn't a serious issue; she was the headstrong mother unable to convince her daughter that she meant business. Pamela—although she didn't admit or even recognize it—had always had the upper hand with Tziporah. It was a kind of love that existed silently between them.

"What's the long face for?" I asked.

My breathing and stride were in rhythm as I watched her reflection. She looked toward the bay and then back at me but said nothing. She carried a paper cup with the Starbucks logo on the side. She was in spandex capris, skintight, with a pink halter top. Her voluptuous figure was the mirror of Tziporah. The sandy-blond hair was that of her father.

I hit the "stop" button, and the treadmill slowed to a walk...and then stopped.

"Don't look so sour," I said in a playful manner. The effect of all that oxygen in my blood was euphoric, but by late afternoon, I would replace it with alcohol.

"I missed my period," she said. "It always comes on the fifteenth."

"Today's the sixteenth," I said.

She'd already spilled coffee on the pink halter.

"Are you serious?" she said. "It's been a month."

Jesus Christ! Now it made sense.

"I took a test," she said. "The one in the blue box. With all those instructions. It said 'positive.'"

I wanted to be angry, accuse her of screwing up the test, but I said nothing. I just stared at her.

"Don't look at me that way," she said. "You're the only one."

"Only?" As soon as I'd heard what I'd said, I wanted it back. But she didn't catch the insult.

"*Only?* Of course not. There was the first time and then some other boy after that. And maybe another one—or two. But that's not the point. My mother's here. I have to tell her."

"Here? At the Dragonfly?"

"No, at the condo."

"Condo? What condo? And why do you have to tell her?"

"Don't look so panic-stricken. I'm the one who's pregnant. And I don't like that I can't call you Nicky."

I stepped down from the treadmill.

"The company owns the condo," she said. "The whole building."

I didn't know whether she meant Lacombe Enterprises owned the building or the law firm owned it. But what difference did it make? Tziporah was here in Hong Kong and not for the shopping.

"You'll meet her tomorrow."

"Meet her?"

"Why are you so jumpy? Yes, we're having dinner with her. Don't worry. I won't tell her yet. Not till it starts to show."

"You're going to go through with it?"

"Of course! I couldn't think of harming—are you serious?"

"I didn't mean it like that. I just...I didn't know."

"She'll think I'm a whore—that's how she'll look at me. Fat lot of room she has to talk. Doing it with her brother. For years! In front of everyone." She looked toward the bay.

"My father won't judge me," she said, still looking toward the ocean. "He won't. He'll smile—I know he will. I can see it now. God, I miss him."

I wanted to comfort her, say something pleasant. I put my arm around her the way I thought her father might.

"Don't ever leave me," she said. "Promise?"

The night rain came down in torrents. It beat down on the canvas awning stretched over the length of the pool and poured over the edges in a steady stream. In the distance were silent flashes of lightning behind dark clouds. Beads of sweat formed on my arms and chest.

"Come," Layonna said. She stood up from the lounge chair we'd been sharing. "Swim with me."

I drained my champagne glass as she tugged me forward by the hand. At the edge of the pool, our waiter said something in Cantonese.

Layonna laughed and answered in English. "So when lightning hit the ocean, all the fish die?"

He had no answer.

Layonna pulled me into the pool in an ungainly splash. She continued to pull me forward, underwater; I watched her underwater smile as I felt guilty for all my anxiety over the upcoming dinner with Tziporah. Part of me wished I'd never shot Meyer in the head, but another part of me knew I might not be alive if I hadn't.

I surfaced to catch my breath. Layonna wrapped her legs around my waist and her arms around my neck. She looked into my face. Her look was serious out of concern.

"You are worried for this business meeting, no?"

I nodded.

"We can leave tomorrow," she said. "In the morning. To Australia and buy this boat. I will teach you the life of sea gypsies."

It was tempting. I could simply disappear. Maybe Pamela wasn't pregnant after all; maybe the pregnancy was made up, a story she *wanted* to be true. But that wasn't Pamela; deceit and guile were not part of her, as they weren't part of her father. They were trusting souls.

I swam to the edge of the pool. Layonna swam underwater and surfaced in front of me. "Come," she said. "Come stay with me tonight. You look tired. Maybe you can tell me of this fight in your heart?"

I pulled myself out of the pool and took a towel from the lounge chair to dry myself. The champagne bottle and my glass were on the end table, but I refused myself another drink.

Layonna slipped a pair of Bermuda shorts and a white T-shirt over her bikini. She removed a pair of canvas slip-on shoes from her bag. I pulled on a pair of cotton pants over my wet underwear and buttoned the front of my shirt.

We took the service elevator down to the ground floor and left the hotel through a back door. The rain had let up at one point but started again in a sudden downpour. Her motor scooter was parked in the rain.

We rode out of the alley and onto the wet streets. Within moments we were drenched in another downpour. We came to a traffic light, and Layonna slowed down to look both ways and then drove through, separating the puddles in long splashes. We drove to the narrow street that led to her apartment, but this time she opened the gate with a remote on her key chain, and we parked in front of her door.

Once we were inside her apartment, my sense of foreboding went away. We dried ourselves with a large towel and changed into robes, and Layonna made green tea. I watched as she heated the water with her back to me. The robe was only inches below her buttocks and far sexier than her bikini. The pale, silky blue robe gave treasure to her nakedness.

I propped pillows against the wall, and we sat back on the futon. A Chinese lantern of red paper hung above the window. The light was soft and peaceful. The tea was calming. My hair was still damp and so was Layonna's. She snuggled close to me.

"Layonna…" I paused. "Before I came to Hong Kong, I killed a man. I looked in his eyes and shot him in the head."

"I know this," she said.

Her fingertips touched my lips to say no more.

Tziporah had insisted our dinner was to be black-tie. She had reserved a section of the restaurant on the first floor of Lacombe Suites. The upper floors were reserved for guests and senior associates there to do business with Chinese industry. Tziporah occupied the penthouse.

The restaurant wasn't the glass and chrome of modern China but comfortable in the baroque cushioned chairs of early Paris, thick carpets, mirrors, and chandeliers with the look of candlelight.

"Remember," Pamela said, "when I introduce you, be nice." The maître d' unhooked a red-velvet rope to let us through and then led the way.

"She looks mean, but she's not. I've gotten her so upset she stutters—then she'll storm off."

We were shown to a table set for four. The maître d' seated Pamela. She wore a shimmering, white, satiny dress with a black sash and Tahitian pearls of charcoal blue. The assistant waiter held my chair out for me.

"I shouldn't do that," she said.

"Do what?"

"Push her buttons. And for God's sake, don't say anything nice about America."

"America?"

"She thinks the whole place is Texas."

"Texas?"

"Uncle Meyer didn't like Texas, so naturally she didn't. Something about oil—it's really boring. You look so handsome. I can't wait for her to meet you."

Our waiter wore a black jacket with red piping; his assistant wore white. The waiter asked if I wished to see the wine list.

"Champagne," I said.

"I'd like that too," said Pamela.

The waiter opened a menu of sparkling wines.

"I don't care!" I said. "Whatever." I was short and abrupt with him, but I didn't mean it. I felt embarrassed, but I didn't apologize. I should have. Pamela didn't seem to notice my rudeness; she was talking about something, explaining something; I didn't hear it. I wanted Tziporah to arrive; I wanted this charade to end.

When the wine came, I made it a point to thank the waiter— perhaps too many times. It gave him the upper hand, the high ground. I saw it in his eyes, the imitation of a gracious nod.

Pamela sat opposite me at the table. Her back was to the entrance. I saw the maître d' unhook the rope to escort Tziporah and Mohammed Algenib to our table. Mohammed was in a tuxedo; Tziporah wore a black dress, sleek-fitting with a low neckline and sleeves. The dress was floor length; the material had an elusive glitter as she walked. She had lost weight since I'd last seen her in Paris, and there was gray in her hair: a white streak in the front and through her temples. She wore a black-velvet ribbon around her throat, snug, with a diamond in the middle.

As she came closer to the table, I stood. The maître d' held Tziporah's chair out, but she didn't sit. She held my eyes in a cold stare. I wanted to look away, but I didn't. I attempted to hold my face without expression.

"Mother, I want you to meet Nicholas Firthwhile."

"Firthwhile," Tziporah repeated, taking her seat. "What an unusual name. How did you come up with it?"

"Come up with it?" Pamela laughed. "It was given to him."

"Yes, indeed," Tziporah said, staring at me, "it was."

Pamela looked at her mother. "You two know each other?" She looked toward me. "Am I missing something here?"

The waiter stood next to Tziporah. He held the champagne bottle in both hands. She nodded, and he filled her glass. Algenib held his hand in polite refusal. The waiter stepped back.

"Tziporah," Algenib said, looking toward her as if for permission to use her first name, "has recently suffered the loss of her brother." He looked at me. "He was found murdered in his library."

"It's still so hard to believe," Pamela said. "Like it didn't happen."

"It did," Tziporah said. "It did." She looked at me. "Are you a man of business, Mr. Firthwhile? It appears you are. You have the look of success—of wealth."

There was something missing in Tziporah's manner. Her eyes weren't quite clear, and she was slower to pronounce a word but not quite. Then it came to me—she was sedated. I'd seen it so often in Adrienne.

"Do they have any idea," Pamela said, "who did it? Is there an investigation?"

"I have no idea," Tziporah said. "They can do what they wish. I'll handle it myself." She looked at me. "In my own way."

"What can you do?" Pamela asked.

Tziporah didn't answer; she was staring at me. "Do you know where Pamela got the black pearls she's wearing?" She didn't look toward Pamela. She was still staring at me. "My brother, Meyer, gave them to her. There was a side of him few people knew. At the kibbutz, as children, I watched him share his food with homeless dogs. They hung around the outskirts, looking for scraps. Meyer took the food from his plate to feed them. He often got into trouble over it. The elders said it encouraged them to hang around. Better to let them turn wild, but Meyer didn't listen."

I didn't see how I could sit through an evening of this. But I wasn't about to bring John Savensworth's name into it. Not with Pamela sitting at the table. I also wanted to mention the innocent people who were killed in the bombing of the King David Hotel, but that would have sounded hollow: a murderer playing peace activist, glib, empty words visible to the heart, and open to silent laughter. Yet another part of me oddly felt the pain in Tziporah's voice, her suffering.

I can't undo it, Tziporah; I can't go back through that door!

"I knew a boy once," she said, "who was asked to do something he couldn't. It was beyond his conscience—so he thought. He was asked to jump from a cliff—with a parachute—but he said he couldn't, and he didn't see why he had to. He had been told that *his rumors* as to the safety of the parachutes were cause enough. Without thinking it through, the boy killed the one who'd asked him to jump. He seemed to think that solved the problem."

There was silence at the table. Algenib looked at me but without judgment. Pamela said nothing, as if she hadn't been following the story. Tziporah asked the waiter for another glass of wine and then looked back at me.

"It wasn't a parachute," I said, "was it?"

She glared at me.

"I heard a similar story," I said. While sitting there I'd finished three glasses of champagne. A third bottle had been opened. My courage to face her came from alcohol.

"In the other vision, the boy wasn't a boy," I continued. "He was a grown man, hardened through false imprisonment. And it wasn't a parachute. He was asked to commit a murder. Told he must. He was even introduced to his intended victim. Why was that? Was there some ridden reason behind it? Some purpose? Since the intended victim was a decent man, the reason had to be quite sadistic—or so selfish it took cruelty to another level."

Tziporah stood. "I won't listen to this!"

There was silence at the table. Pamela looked from her mother to me. "What's going on?" she asked. "Is this some kind of game?" She looked at Algenib. He avoided her eyes.

Tziporah stepped from the table. Algenib stood next to her. She turned to leave.

Several steps away she stopped and looked back at me, her eyes rimmed with tears and filled with hate.

The night I had confessed the murder of Meyer Lacombe, the night we rode Layonna's motor scooter through heavy rain, leaned against pillows in her apartment, listening to the rain in the flooding streets beneath black clouds scudding across a lighter sky, Layonna described the reason her father had murdered a man. He had cut his throat, attached weights to his body, and pushed him overboard, far out at sea.

"This man was there to earn his rice," she said. "It is what we all do. What we must do to live. But he doesn't listen to my father. He only waits for him to stop so he can talk. He doesn't hear a thing. The kind of man who sees a child with no foot, no leg, and this does not move him to sadness. That people have problems, they suffer, is invisible to him. They think of themselves like they are blind to the world. You know this kind of man?"

I nodded. They're the self-absorbed who interpret their con-descension as an act of kindness—intelligent enough not to bring overt attention to their self-perceived acts of kindness, while their transparent lives are shallow and rehearsed to their audience. Yes, I know them; I've lunched with them.

"This man say my father must pay new tax. Buy license for this tax. He show papers of authority. They are written in Mandarin. My father laugh. This is a joke—pay tax to fish far out at sea. The man say government own the sea, the fish. My father lose patience—he chase him off, tell him not to come back. The man is now angry. Say he will come back with government police. Say he have authority of Beijing. He will take my father's boat. He promise this. My father say he will see him dead first."

At this time her father's boat was docked in the estuary with the other boat families, boats they lived on, worked from, fished from. The sea gypsies gathered in the many estuaries during the height of the monsoon season.

Her father didn't take this agent seriously, this man who claimed the government owned all the fish in the sea. "The sea of all things," her father had said. The vastness of it! But this kind of man wouldn't back down; he had to save face. He too, no doubt, would lie awake at night replaying the insults exchanged between the two men. Insults in front of witnesses who'd made judgments, taken sides, thought the agent was without honor. To be insulted, spoken to like that by a gypsy! A Tanka! He wouldn't tolerate it. He would seize that boat.

"Days later, in heavy rain, the agent man return. My mother and father have lunch then, under the boat canopy. Rain pours off the roof, over the sides, but we are dry. The rice steams; my mother cuts small pieces of fish to add to it. I am only a little girl then. I am not thinking of what will happen. There is a boy I see on another boat. He is my age maybe. I watch him. I think it would be nice to touch him, to learn how to kiss. I think of ways to be nice for him, but he makes mean faces at me, sticks his tongue out, but still I like him.

"Then I see the agent man. He is coming in the rain, walking through mud. There are two men with him. Men in uniform, with guns. They come to our boat. My father stands up, tells them to leave. But the agent man steps onto our boat. My father yells angry words at him. The men in uniform stand watching, holding guns. Behind them boat people have gathered. The agent man speaks first in Cantonese, then Mandarin. My father doesn't speak Mandarin. No boat people speak this. My father tells my mother in Portuguese to take me inside the boat. But I can still see; I watch this happen.

"The agent man takes papers from leather case, pushes them against my father—tell him our boat now belong to the People's Republic. The boat people step forward—some hold thick bamboo; the air is nervous.

"The agent man push my father back with papers in his fist. My father stumble; he reach down to catch his balance. He finds the fish knife my mother use, on the table. The agent man laughs when he sees the knife. In Cantonese he tells the police to arrest my father and take the boat. My father plunges the knife into his chest. The agent man stares at him with wild eyes; he doesn't believe this happened. The boat people beat the police with bamboo before they move. My father pull the knife from the man's chest and cut his throat. He let him bleed onto the deck. One of the police is still alive, but the boat people hold his head underwater..."

The boat people then made their boats ready, Layonna said, secured their belongings, and headed out to sea in the heavy rain of the monsoon. Several days later they dispersed from the open ocean. Many of them found harbor in the estuaries south of Macau. They left no fingerprint in defense of their lives, their way of life, their genetic lineage portrayed in superstition, folklore, and oral history.

The rain had let up as water dripped from the eves above the open window, with the faint glow of the moon through thinning clouds. Layonna lay next to me as I leaned back against the wall, against the pillows. She lay with her head and cheek next to my chest. I felt her warmth through the silky blue robe.

"Yes," she said. "I know this look."

I received a phone call the day after my dinner engagement with Tziporah. The caller spoke with a Cantonese accent and with the aplomb of bureaucratic authority. I was "requested" to appear at the Immigration Tower, 7 Gloucester Road, with my passport and visa by one in the afternoon. "No later, Mr. Fluffwell."

"Can you tell me what this concerns?"

"One o'clock, Mr. Fluffwell." There was finality in his tone.

The name Firthwhile and the British passport I traveled under had been provided to me by Meyer Lacombe. The name was bogus, but that was of little concern to me. (I had become accustomed to—even fond of—the name.) It was the passport that now concerned me. How deeply must you scratch the surface to see the nonexistence of Nicholas Firthwhile?

A British national, as I appeared to be, was allowed to stay in Hong Kong for 180 days without a visa. In the beginning I hadn't imagined any reason to request an extension, but I was now four and a half months into my stay. I had planned to finish my financial affairs in a week, maybe two, and then leave. Layonna had never been imagined, not in all my fantasies, dreams, or even hopes. She was in the realm of Shakespeare, Helen of Troy, an underwater image—not quite real—yet the mere thought of losing her brought panic to my heart.

Layonna was in the restaurant at the hotel; her morning shift had just begun. She brought me coffee and a warm croissant.

"I have no idea what they want," I said.

"I have been there," she said. "They ask for birth certificate. Papers to show I am citizen. But I have none. They are from Beijing. Hong Kong people must take orders from them."

"If you have no birth certificate—"

"They know before they ask this. They do not like sea gypsies. It is to let me know they do not like me. It is a game. They called three times to play this game. I go there, and it is the same. Behind a face of business, they laugh at me."

My summons to appear before them was no game. It was instigated, controlled, directed by the hand of Meyer Lacombe reaching out from the grave. Tziporah.

"Why are you drinking so early?" Pamela asked. She had arrived at my suite without notice, knocked once, and tried to open the door, but it was locked. She had become impatient waiting for me to answer and knocked again, harder. I went to the door.

"Mother's very curious about you. She had all kinds of questions."

"It's not early." I put the cork back in the wine bottle.

"It's not even noon."

"What kind of questions?"

"What you do for a living…but she wasn't serious about it. I could tell. It was more like she wanted to know what *I* knew. She asked if there was anything between us. Anything she should know."

"What did you tell her?"

"About what? Us?"

"Anything. What did you tell her?"

"Don't bite my head off," she said.

"Sorry…I'm a little edgy. I have a meeting at Immigration. In about an hour."

"Why?" She laughed. "Are they going to deport you?"

"Don't laugh—they might."

"What on earth for? You're kidding, right?"

"What did she say? Your mother…about me?"

I poured another glass of wine, which I knew was a mistake. I needed a clear head for the interview at Immigration. I had to make sense; my answers had to hold together—sobriety and truth, but truth was out of the question.

"I'll go with you," Pamela said.

"With me?"

"It looks more respectable. More legitimate if you have a wife."

"The immigration office? Not a good idea. No."

"Too bad I'm not showing." She placed her hands on her stomach. "They'd be extra nice, I bet."

"No, Pamela. You're not going."

⚊⧏ ⧐⚊

The heart of Hong Kong, the business-commercial-authoritarian face, is unimaginative glass and steel with concrete made to look like Egyptian stone (here and there a pyramid atop a rectangle, the Egyptian sarcophagus upside down); the verisimilitude of a crawling anthill; the *Star Trek* version of the Borg, where the individual is eliminated, where even the thought *individual* is blasphemy.

I took a cab through this shiny light-reflecting wasteland to Immigration Tower. When I had been on the phone with the person who had called, I didn't think to ask for a name; I'd been too taken by surprise.

I stopped at a reception desk on the upper floors and gave my name. A young woman with straight, chin-length hair, parted in the center, looked up at me. I repeated my name.

"Nicholas Firthwhile. I have a meeting at one o'clock with…I'm not sure."

She asked me to spell the name while she slowly traced her finger down a list in front of her. There were only three names listed using the Latin alphabet; the rest were in Chinese.

"Mr. Fluffwell?"

"Yes."

She picked up the phone, held it to her ear for a moment as if waiting for someone to answer, and then announced my arrival in English, for my benefit no doubt. Perhaps my uneasiness was that visible, and she was bored. She hung up and asked me to please be seated, a faint smile of amusement on her face.

I had my passport and a replica of a birth certificate from the United Kingdom but no driver's license, no other photo ID.

Within several minutes a man came through the office doorway behind the receptionist and out to the waiting room. He was in his late forties perhaps, the puffiness of middle age gathering in little pockets under his eyes; his hair was stiff and greasy, pushed in place, not combed; and his white shirt appeared as though it had been worn for several days. He also wore a red tie.

"Mr. Firthwhile?" He spoke with little or no accent at all; he wasn't the one who had called earlier on the phone. He turned back toward the office he had just left and, at the same time, indicated but didn't say aloud that I was to follow him.

As I passed the receptionist, she glanced up at me with a half smile of pleasure at my discomfort.

I followed the man into the office and was offered a seat, an open hand indicating a chair next to his desk. His desk was neither sloppy nor orderly: a few paper clips scattered, an open stapler waiting for staples, a pair of scissors, a few papers shuffled. He clearly was a man no longer concerned with advancement, having been passed over not through lack of ability but nepotism—the resignation of a faceless expression as he took a seat behind his desk, with retirement a waited-for daydream.

Off to the side, at a desk near the window, a younger man watched. From the small smile, I imagined he was the voice on the phone earlier that morning. He was in his early thirties perhaps, with short hair, tousled with an askew eye to style, the look of a trainee waiting to be in charge, to become the face of bureaucratic authority, imagined or created, self-serving.

"Mr. Firthwhile, your passport, please." At no point did he offer his name, and I didn't ask. We both knew the outcome, the order he had received, which neither names nor protest would change. "And your visa…"

"Visa? But I'm…" His look stopped me. The futility of my response was to be pitied. We knew the game, yet I continued. "…a British National. I have a hundred and…" I trailed off; it was silly to continue. Like an actor long tired of his part, rehearsals, performances, I handed him the passport.

"We will this keep for now." He looked at the passport for a moment and then at me. "There's nothing more," he said. "You can go."

As I left the office, past the slight smirk of the man near the window, I imagined the phone call the immigration agent had received from an office without a face, the hum of factories, the entanglement of deals, the smell of crude oil, interest impending, and promissory notes. The call would have come from Paris to Dubai, to Beijing, to Hong Kong, to a tired bureaucrat waiting for retirement.

Tziporah was now in her later years. The voluptuous figure of her youth had grown soft, and her skin no longer had the elasticity of a woman in her twenties, thirties, even fifties but was now spongy beneath the surface. By no means, however, did she appear old. Her estrogen may have come to rest but not her sexuality. Men in their fifties watched appreciatively as she walked, still with the sway of promise, the flow of a satiny bedsheet rippling across the mattress, settling to the surface. This genetic good fortune was passed on to Pamela but not the guile, the single-mindedness of revolt against any imagined or real obstacle in her path. Mother and daughter were somehow bewildered by each other. Pamela's youth and her father's nature sheltered her from Tziporah's demand for decorum, while Tziporah was left frustrated, speechless in the face of Pamela's mischievous, often childlike, sometimes sly teasing.

Pamela and her father were not judgmental souls, although for Pamela, her home environment had been unknown, unnamed, until the time of puberty, when the meaning of sex and its function in our lives became clear. By then, however, it had been imprinted since birth: Tziporah and Meyer arising each morning from the same bed as though incest and reality had been raised as lion and lamb from infancy.

⊫╪ ╪⊧

Since Tziporah's arrival in Hong Kong, Pamela visited her mother every day. She went by cab from the Dragonfly to Lacombe Suites. Algenib was always there during Pamela's visits and escorted her back to the Dragonfly, where he also stayed, just down the hall from me.

"I like going there," Pamela said. "She's funny in an old-fashioned way." She was in my suite, her hand on the refrigerator door. "I'm hungry for ice cream…" She turned toward me. "Yet she's not old-fashioned. Not really. She's forward thinking…Now where did *that* come from? *Forward thinking.* Sounds like my father. You have to meet him. I know you'll like him." She closed the refrigerator door. "Take me out for ice cream."

"You can get it downstairs. Or call for it."

"You're no fun."

"What did she ask about—your mother?"

"Mostly you. And that girl downstairs. The mermaid."

"What did you tell her?"

"About you? Actually not much. She agrees, though, that you seem to have money. What do you do anyway?"

"I went to law school. Practiced a short time in London."

"Where did you get your money? You inherit it? Marry into it?"

"I'm not married."

"But you were…right?"

"Divorced," I lied. "She was English and older than me."

"Mother said something funny. Said you look like you've been in prison." She laughed. "You wouldn't last a minute in prison."

192

I poured a glass of wine, but I didn't offer any to Pamela, and I knew instantly the reason I didn't. She was pregnant, and the child she was carrying was mine. The thought was eerie, unnerving, yet protective.

"Why'd she ask about the mermaid?"

"I don't know." She shrugged as if to herself. "Maybe Mohammed was talking about her. I saw him with her. Outside the hotel. You know she has a red motor scooter?"

"Algenib?"

"Yes. Don't know why. It wasn't like he was hitting on her. Not unless she grew a penis."

"What were they talking about?"

"I don't know. She's interesting, though—in a mystical way. Even when she walks. A certain grace and balance that flows. Yet when I look at her, I think, *What kind of man would she attract...or could attract?* She looks so..." She thought for a moment. "...unattainable."

To Pamela, Layonna was a sylph, a fairy tale apart from life. She could have found me in Layonna's embrace and thought it no more real than pixie dust.

—+ +—

There were bookshelves made with red bricks stacked at the ends of long boards, four shelves high. The books were of a practical nature and romantic: *The Ancient Art of Chinese Healing*, *The Craft of Herbs and Seaweed*, the poetry of Du Fu, Li Po, *Women Poets of China*, and *The Nature of Green Tea*.

Layonna removed a book from one of the shelves. "These are many poems of love," she said, "by women. A woman loves different than a man. Her love is soft. It is her nature. She brings more life into the world."

She got up from the mat where she had been sitting cross-legged, to make tea. She put the water on to boil and then turned toward me, as if in thought, but said nothing, still in thought. She then prepared and filled two white cups with green tea. I held the cups while she sat again on the mat with me. She straightened her legs and sat facing me, her legs touching mine.

"Why did you kill this man who haunts you?"

I stared at her for a moment: the straightforwardness of her question left me without an answer. She sipped her tea, her eyes still on me.

"He held power over me," I said, "and ordered me to kill another man. A man I liked—I do like."

"So he killed himself, this man you killed."

Her words were simple—without the stage makeup of morality—the black-and-white sense of behavior laid bare.

"This young woman at the hotel," she said. "She is part of this story, no? She holds part of your heart. I see it when she looks at you—she doesn't know I am your lover."

"Layonna—"

She stopped my words with her fingertips.

"In ancient China the emperor had many wives but one favorite. The other wives were jealous—but my love is more. We will have this boat together. You will do what you must."

Her fingertips went from my lips to my temple. She kissed me while looking into my eyes.

Tziporah requested my presence. She wished to have lunch with me. The invitation came through Mohammed Algenib; he approached me in the fitness center. I was on the treadmill, running at a brisk pace, facing the glass wall overlooking the harbor. I saw his reflection in the rain-spotted glass. Once he was through the doorway—the glass-door closing behind him—he stopped, removed a white hanky from his back pocket, and coughed into it. I'd seen him do this in the past, several times, but of late it seemed more frequent. He folded the hanky back into his pocket and then hesitated, as if waiting for another cough, but there was nothing. He continued toward me.

I slowed the treadmill to a walk as he got closer, and before he spoke, I stopped it.

"Tziporah—" He reached quickly for his hanky to cover his mouth and coughed. It went on for a moment, and then he apologized, saying he believed it was a cold. "Tziporah wishes to speak with you." He refolded the hanky but didn't replace it in his pocket;

he held it in his hand. "The lounge in the atrium. One o'clock this afternoon."

He turned to leave; there was no hesitation in his movement, no moment for me to ask why or what this was about. Although the invitation was polite and contained a sense of decorum, it was a command nonetheless.

One o'clock. The hour when the lounge opened, the hour when Layonna arrived for her shift. The lounge was never crowded at this time. Only one waitress was required.

It had been six weeks since Pamela had discovered she was pregnant. No physical changes were noticeable. Her weight and figure appeared the same, and she mentioned nothing of morning sickness, but her moods were less predictable. She might call on the phone to complain about her mother or lament that she didn't have enough alone time, while resisting my hint to hang up so she could have "alone time." She might tell me an anecdote concerning her mother and then end it by saying, "Can you believe that?" I could picture her shaking her head, an amusement that contained a silent respect for her mother's strength and her mother's deliberate inability to disguise her love.

"She might scold me, and then I'd notice, from the corner of my eye, a little smile. I knew early on I'd get my way. That doesn't mean I don't love her. I do—even the last time…when she told me to get out of her hair. She was really upset that day. 'You're driving me nuts,' she said. I can't remember what I did. 'Go visit your father. Go to China!' That's when I got on the plane. It was actually just a prank, but I ended up pregnant.

"Did I tell you this before? Not the pregnant part; obviously you know that. About how I got to China?"

Layonna awoke early each day. Even as a little girl on her father's boat, docked within the forested reaches of the estuary during the monsoon season. She told of rainy mornings in the warmth of the cabin, lying in her bed, hearing the rain strike the water and the bamboo-and-wicker roof woven so tightly that the rain poured in rivulets over the edges, while her father repaired his nets under a canopy stretched over the back. Her mother made tea from seaweed as Layonna sat watching her father and sipped her morning tea.

It had rained that morning—the afternoon I was to meet Tziporah—as Layonna sipped green tea from the comfort of her futon, watching the rain drip from the leaves of the trees. I tried to picture her: her legs drawn up close to her chest, her white tea-cup held in both hands, as she looked out through the open window with the smell of rain and the dark clouds moving above the trees. She may have taken a book from the shelves near the futon. I would guess it was a book of poetry, perhaps the truth and beauty of Du Fu:

> *Leaving the audience by the quiet corridors,*
> *Stately and beautiful, we pass through the Palace gates,*
>
> *Turning in different directions: you go to the West*
> *With the Ministers of State; I, otherwise.*
>
> *On my side, the willow-twigs are fragile, greening.*
> *You are struck by scarlet flowers over there.*
>
> *Our separate ways! You write so well, so kindly,*
> *To caution, in vain, a garrulous old man.*

After reading for a time, she would have replaced the book on the shelf as her fingertips lingered a moment longer on its spine.

She might have eaten a rice cake with a second cup of tea, brushed her hair, applied a faint, almost flesh-colored lipstick, and then still, a moment longer, looked into the mirror, not with thoughts of herself but of the poetry she'd just read.

By noon the heavy rain would have let up, only to reappear again and then fade to a misty drizzle. It was the pattern of the day, and the evening to come.

Closer to one o'clock, she would have taken a plastic rain jacket from the closet and pulled the hood over her hair. The red motor scooter was in front of her apartment, locked at the wheel and covered with clear plastic. She'd shake the water from the plastic covering, fold it, and place it in the small storage box mounted on the back. A turn of the ignition key would bring the electric motor silently to life.

In less than thirty minutes, she'd lay eyes on Tziporah—aging consort to dead pharaohs—while Tziporah watched this lissome, sylph-like creature approach our table.

The atrium had a pond with flowery fish, like an impression-
ist painting underwater, and dwarf palms along the edge, reflected in the pond, and hanging ferns and philodendrons with
long tendrils touching the water, and daylight through the tall
ceiling glass. The tables were covered with white tablecloths and
wineglasses turned upside down and folded white napkins with
iridescent dragonflies embroidered at the corners. At the center
of each table was an unlit candle in a clear globe.

I arrived before Tziporah, who was escorted by Mohammed
Algenib to the lounge. He wore a white shirt open at the neck and
a camel-colored blazer. She said something to him at the entrance,
and then he departed with a slight bow of the head. His devotion
to her was beyond anything I'd ever seen.

Tziporah looked at me across the empty lounge and then came
toward my table. She wore a black dress, the hem to her knees,
and no jewelry. The diamond-clustered ring she usually wore on
her left hand was missing. I stood to greet her. I felt drawn to her
at that moment; she emanated the same charm that drew me to

Meyer, left me vulnerable, looking to please him as one wishes to please those with power and wealth. But there was a presence in Tziporah that went beyond the glow of wealth. There was a sexuality that could destroy a man's soul, and even though you knew the danger, you couldn't pull away.

I held a chair out for her. My punctilio might have seemed like a charade, but it wasn't. Even though my tears were unseen, I wanted her forgiveness.

Without looking at me, she accepted my offer and took her seat. She looked around for a server, but none was in sight. She then caught the attention of a young man in a white apron with stains on the front. She signaled him to the table and asked for champagne. He said he would send our waitress immediately.

"No," she said. "I want it now. You bring it."

He started to speak, but she cut him off. "I don't care what kind. Just bring it." She waved the back of her hand as though she were shooing a fly from the table.

The silence was awkward.

Moments later the young man returned with the champagne and an ice bucket in a stand. He had changed his apron. Tziporah noticed; her eyes went from the apron to his face. He avoided her glance and filled our glasses.

She tasted the champagne and set the glass back on the table. There was no lipstick on the glass.

"Adrienne has cancer," she said. "Lung cancer." She looked at me. "That's her name, isn't it?"

I cleared my throat. "Yes. How—"

"Graham is engaged. A German girl. Nadine."

"Are they—"

"In South Africa? Yes. You've been divorced for more than a year now. Did you know that? Of course not. You've been busy."

She raised her champagne glass to her lips and then looked around as though she were expecting someone.

"What's the point of this?" I asked. "This meeting. You want the money back?"

"Money…and what does that do, Nicholas? Resurrect the dead?"

I don't know why I'd said that—a way perhaps to reference what I'd done without mentioning Meyer's name.

"Are you going to kill me? Is that why you're here?" I heard my tone, the humility; it made her look at me.

"Pamela is pregnant," she said.

"She told you?"

"Of course not. You think I can't see it, that I wouldn't know?"

I looked for something to say—through all the questions I had rehearsed—while from the corner of my eye, I saw orange-and-gray fish with plumelike fins, a fairy tale underwater.

"Why so much?" I said. I looked up at Tziporah. "Why nine million? It's an odd number."

"He liked you, Nicholas." Her tone was soft with memory. "He did."

"Then why prison?"

"That was me. I saw you as a threat. But not soon enough."

"Why are you here?"

"To hand you the bill," she said. "To collect what you owe."

The moment was then broken. Layonna appeared, coming across the room toward our table. Behind her, in the near distance, the young man in the white apron watched as though he had given her fair warning of the woman with dark-crystal eyes.

Tziporah looked at me. "She's quite lovely, Nicholas. Are you going to miss her?"

Tziporah had said this same thing to me one other time, so had Marcel Gordon. When I later remembered this, recalled their faces, the tone that each had conveyed, perhaps unknowingly, I felt like a fool yet a little wiser, however late that wisdom may have come.

Meyer had summoned me to another meeting, a late breakfast at his penthouse, as Marcel Gordon had referred to it when he had delivered the message. For some reason I had taken it for granted that the meeting was between Meyer and me. I hadn't expected, anticipated in any way, that Tziporah would make a surprise, casual entrance.

There was a breakfast table near the balcony but not on the balcony. The sliding glass doors to the balcony were closed, with the curtains drawn open to a gray morning of chill mist. In the distance were the remnants of a morning fog, wispy along the horizon.

Meyer was seated at the table in a long robe of maroon satin with a black paisley print. He wore leather slippers; his bare ankles and shins, with a few lonely black hairs, were exposed. When I was shown in, he held a butter knife in his left hand and toast in the other. He waved me forward with the butter knife. "Come in, Nicholas. Please have a seat."

As I took a seat, he asked in a pleasant tone, "Coffee? It's my own blend. I crafted it." He smiled. "A mixture of Columbian, dark Italian roast, and few beans from Kenya."

It was his way of letting me know, although perhaps not consciously, that he controlled everything: coffee, oil, shipping lanes, and most certainly the individual lives of those around him. But his formula for success wasn't to be divulged, shared, or publicized. He might have truly liked me (I don't know and don't want to know, for conscience's sake), but the thought that he held an undefined fatherly love for me, the kind of love that comes through intricate chemistry, not time spent together, was the betrayal of his own heart. Tziporah knew this, sensed it through an intuition that lay only in the female heart—an insight that is oblivious to men—while she watched, helplessly, as though dark clouds were threatening her soul.

Meyer spoke at first of my contributions to the law firm. Although I had done nothing of importance (singed a form, approved this or that, all of which were in French), I accepted the praise while knowing it was undeserved—but who turns down the warm glow of a compliment?

A silver coffeepot was set at the center of the table. Meyer reached for it, poured my coffee, his finger holding the lid down as he tilted the spout forward, and then looked at me. "Tell me what you think."

It was my turn to give a compliment. I sipped carefully; steam rose from the cup.

"It's wonderful." I took another sip. "Rich…smooth…It truly is."

"*I* thought so," he said. "I should turn my hand to wine." He said this in a light manner, but he believed it; he believed it in the way one might secretly believe he's right and the world isn't quite up to speed. These people hold a special knowledge—a knowledge that must be protected from criticism or ridicule. It was this very same inner conviction that led Meyer to believe that once John Savensworth was out of the way, Pamela would come to love him as her only true father. He could see this, and I had to be made to see it—*me*, this imagined, invisible sibling to Pamela.

"Your grandfather," he said, spreading jam on his toast, "the Hungarian Jew." He looked up at me. "He was an exceptional craftsman. Did you know that?" He indicated, with a tilt of his head, the far wall, but he didn't look that way. "The rolltop desk. He made that."

I looked at the desk. "How—"

"Did I get it?" Meyer completed for me. "You aren't the only one who digs into the past."

The mood at the table was both intimate and dangerous, as though bare fingertips were playing with razor blades. But when Tziporah entered the room unexpectedly, the mood parted like a curtain to let in a new, different kind of light: softer, without masculine pride at the perimeter, but silently cunning and patient. She had just finished her morning bath and was wrapped in a robe that matched Meyer's, her hair still damp, scented; her makeup yet to be applied; the subtle swish of her robe as she came barefoot across the carpet; Meyer smiling at her as she approached. Instinctively I stood, ready to hold a chair out for her: Tziporah, looking at me, though not directly, deeply seductive in her sixties—Cleopatra without need of makeup.

I slid the chair forward as Tziporah seated herself. Without looking at me, she poured a cup of coffee and reached for a slice of toast. "Well," she said, still not acknowledging me, "what did I miss?"

Her robe parted when she deliberately crossed her legs, and the material fell away. Her olive skin was without a hair follicle or sign of age. The tilt of her head acknowledged my notice.

"How's work?" she asked, while Meyer refilled his coffee cup. "International law—do you find it to your liking?"

"I believe his mind is elsewhere," Meyer said. "The desk."

"What do you think of it?" she said. "Beautiful, isn't it? There isn't anything a Jew can't do once he sets his mind to it."

"How long have you had it?" I asked.

"I'd say a year," Meyer said, with the smile of pride. "About the time you took an unusual interest in me."

"He was trying to please his father-in-law," Tziporah added. "English aristocracy." She looked at me. "Quite above your station. Don't you think?"

Meyer said nothing, although there was a smile of delight in his eyes. Tziporah held a piece of toast as though she were about to take a bite, and without looking at me, she asked, "Are you going to miss her?"

I looked at Meyer and then back at her.

"Adrienne," Tziporah said. "That's her name, isn't it?"

"I don't understand."

"It's a simple question. Are you going to miss her?"

When I'd returned to my Paris office, Pauline wasn't there. Her sweater was over the back of her chair, and soft music was coming from her desk drawer, which was just slightly open. I left my office door open so I could see her when she returned. Fifteen or twenty minutes later, she still hadn't returned. There was nothing specific I needed. I simply wanted her company, the sweet innocence of naïveté, a comfort needed after a morning far more unsettling than I could have imagined.

I saw Marcel enter the outer office. He said he'd thought he'd "pop in" to see how things were going—"*voir comment les choses allaient*"—which at the time meant nothing to me. The French language still had the sound of unknown music to my ear.

"Have you seen Pauline?" I asked.

He looked over his shoulder with feigned surprise. "She isn't here?"

"She must have stepped out," I said. "I thought you'd know."

He shook his head as if to say, *What a shame; she isn't here.* He turned to leave and then stopped and turned back toward my office.

In a less ironic, less harmless tone, full of past grievance, he asked, "Are you going to miss her?"

Months later I was in the maximum-security wing of La Santé Prison.

Torture is still part of Chinese culture. The ability to imagine the pain in the tissue and flesh of another soul—in any mammal at all—is lost behind medieval eyes. Disfigurement means nothing to the blind. Chinese prisons are notorious for this, among the worst in the world, and the Tanka often have experienced it.

"My uncle had no money," Layonna said. "He stole nothing. He come ashore to trade dry fish for rice. But he was arrested."

We were in a section of old Hong Kong—not the tourist traps but an area forgotten by time. Colored awnings of oiled cloth stretched from the fronts of shops to cover the space above the sidewalks, as rickshaws moved hesitantly through the crowded streets, stopping for pedestrians. Firecrackers snapped in the air as sulfurous smoke drifted from the front of a shop that sold toys and fireworks and newspapers in Cantonese. As a fair-skinned Caucasian, I drew notice, even more so walking next to Layonna.

We stopped at a tiny shop for tea and rice cakes shaped like cookies. There were only four tables inside, a mere cubbyhole with a view of the street. The rice cakes were served with green tea.

They were sweet and round and tasted pleasantly of coconut and sugar.

"What were the charges?" I asked. "Why did they arrest him?"

She watched me bite into the cake. "You like the sweet, no? I will make them for you." The sincerity of her smile, as clear as a blue sky, touched me like nothing ever had before. I wanted to crawl inside her to see the world through her eyes.

She refilled our cups from a porcelain-like teapot and then looked at me as if still considering my question.

"He is from my father's side. He too looks Indian. This was part of the reason to arrest him. The police, all from Beijing, do not like Indians, Portuguese, and the English. They are from a time when Chinese were treated like slaves. Beijing is very proud, and still think like the ancients. Beijing is a *new* emperor."

My love of green tea seemed to have come from nowhere, as my love for Layonna had—suddenly, without reason or thought.

"You like this tea," she said. "I see that."

"Yes..." There was a long silence as we looked at each other... but her thoughts were somewhere else, further ahead of mine.

"You must be careful," she said. "If you are arrested, I never see you again."

"What happened to him?"

"They say he must pay taxes to sell fish, but he have no money—that is why he wish to trade. But they don't listen. They say it is against the law to have no money. Because we are Tanka, they do this. The new emperor is embarrassed for the world to know sea gypsies are here. It is not modern."

"Is he still in prison? Is he alive?"

"No, he escape. He hide in sewer garbage, buried for three days. When trucks haul it out, he is free. He has never returned to land. But he has all the scars of torture. That is why you must leave Hong Kong, my Nicholas. If this woman wish to put you there, you must leave."

"But I have no passport. I'm not even sure what's happening."

"They lock him in a box made of iron bars. Chain his wrists to the bars, his ankles to the back. They leave him this way for months. They sew his lips together with string, leave room only for a straw. He escape like this. My mother cut the string. You can still see the scars."

The mental image of the iron-bar box and the man's mouth sewn shut was sickening. How could anyone watch this, let alone do it to another person?

"Do you have—"

"Yes." She removed a two-ounce plastic bottle of vodka from her straw bag. I emptied it into my tea.

"We must leave," she said. "My father can take us from here. You wish Australia? He can do this."

But I had no passport. Neither did Layonna; she didn't even have a country, only the sea—a floating tribe and an oral history. But she could present herself to Australia, the United States, Great Britain, Canada, or France without a passport and not cause great suspicion or apprehension. Her gender and her beauty, her lissome quality, intellect, and many languages would grant her access to the Western world. But I was another story: a Westerner with a fingerprint history of education, prison, and a double identity would be seen as fair game to the politically ambitious.

"Are you trying to avoid me?" Pamela turned toward the refrigerator. "God, I miss champagne."

Pamela had let herself into my suite; somehow she now had an access card. I otherwise might have asked how she had gotten it and why, but she was my line of communication with Tziporah without the face-to-face distraction of underlying hatred.

"Did you see the fighting on the news?" she asked. "The Jews and Arabs again. Or are they Palestinians? What's the difference anyway? It's like a brother and sister having a really nasty fight," she said, pulling open the refrigerator door.

"Buy me some fake champagne," she said, looking inside the refrigerator: three bottles of wine, a block of cheddar cheese, and an empty egg carton.

"Fizzy grape juice or something." She straightened up. "I miss getting buzzed with you."

She pressed her hips close to my groin, with her arms around my neck, as she looked into my eyes. She moved her hips from side to side and up and down. "Do you miss me? You never call. You disappear for days."

She pressed her face to the side of my neck in true affection. Thoughts of her father ran through me, the elegance of an uncorrupted soul, while just inches away the art of creation was taking place in her womb.

She kissed me on the lips, quickly, and then, interrupted by a thought, she said, "You can't find a movie here. It's all that karate crap. Girl in a chop-your-head-off pose, suddenly jumping, like, a mile or running up the side of a wall. Give me a break." Her arms went from around my neck to my waist. "I miss England. And real movies. *Bridget Jones's Diary*...the good stuff."

She was homesick, and her life had been turned upside down, reorganized, placed in different corners, and although she wasn't one to whine, it must have been unsettling as her hormones played dice with her mood.

"Go home and change," I said. "I'll take you out to dinner."

She looked at me. "Thank you." Her eyes were glassy; for a moment I thought she was going to cry. "Come get me when you're ready."

When she had gone, I stared at the door she had just closed behind her. I felt ashamed for not having understood Adrienne's torment. To be a woman must be an internal maze of thrones and roses.

I showered, shampooed and dried my hair, and chose a navy blazer that had been tailored for me. It wasn't the work of Peterus (nothing could be), but it was a good fit. The silk-and-wool weave was Parisian to my fingertips.

When I stopped at Pamela's suite, the door was a few inches open. Lily of the Valley, an English perfume, drifted from inside. I tapped once on the door and went in. She stepped from the bedroom while attaching an earring. She wore navy slacks, well-tailored to her hips. Her blouse was a silky fuchsia that came straight down, held forward by her full breasts. She wore a thin diamond necklace with the sparkle of luxury. A change was taking place. The teenager in love was becoming a mother raised in privilege and fathered by a future Nobel laureate.

As a child Layonna played hide-and-seek with other children in the estuaries during monsoon season. They ran in the rain, looking to hide behind a tree, in the back of a bush, or up a tree—the seeker peeking through spread fingers covering her face, the others screeching as the counter neared ten. They ran barefoot through squishy mud, their legs spattered, and squealed with delight when they were discovered.

The sea provided both food and refuge. Fathers and brothers, uncles and older cousins provided constant repair to their boats and the gear that harvested their living. Layonna's mother watched, glanced up from her work to see her husband: this handsome man with thick black hair, as he pulled the cord taut through a mended sail. Inside the cabin her daughter read books in Portuguese, Hindustani, and Cantonese—books of poetry, Chinese history, and the life of Buddha, their pages protected in waterproof containers.

When the clouds parted long enough for the sun to sparkle off the water, the children swam in the river and dove from the bows of the boats; a somersault soon perfected, a back dive, a reverse dive with a double somersault. "I dare you to do it," they taunted one another. "Bet you can't!"

"Bet I can."

The parting clouds were short lasting as the rains came in torrents. Layonna was called back to the boat, but she and her friends wanted to play, even though she was shivering; her lips were turning blue. Her mother called out to her. Reluctantly, as though disaster had struck, she was torn from her play and returned to the boat. Her mother dried her hair, mildly scolding that she had been too long in the water, kissing the top of her daughter's head. Layonna held a steamy cup of hot water flavored with lemon, a tea leaf, and bits of lemon zest on the surface.

Early in their history, the sea gypsies ventured far out to sea. The warmth of the southern waters drew them forward for months at a time. Their navigation was a compass through the South China Sea, past the Philippines, as they kept land in distant sight, and then Celebes Sea, winding through the islands of Indonesia, Papua, the Banda and Arafura Seas to northern Australia and the estuaries east of Darwin. The weather was always a concern. Purplish-gray and white clouds rolled across the sky with patches of brilliant blue and fierce sunshine burning through, only to change minutes later.

Not until modern times was the threat of piracy through Indonesian waters a reality. At the first sign of trouble, the gypsies pulled their boats together, fastened with ropes to form a single boat adrift, while the pirates approached in power craft. One day, when this happened, Layonna was sent into the cabin and out of sight.

There was nothing of value aboard the gypsy boats, and the pirates knew it. For them it was an amusement to humiliate, rape, or perhaps murder one of the men in a show of bravado. The pirates, a band of six or seven armed men, pulled alongside the few wooden boats tied together and boarded these "pieces of junk." The gypsies bowed and fawned, feigned humility and fear—"Please don't hurt us"—while their Japanese swords were concealed within easy reach.

From where Layonna lay hidden, she heard sudden screams, war cries, and a burst of gunfire. It lasted but a minute, and then silence, and the eerie groans of dying men, their limbs and organs severed. When Layonna appeared from the cabin, she saw bloody corpses dropped overboard, her father holding a blood-covered sword as long as a man's arm. Corpses and expanding pools of blood drifted on the water's surface as holes were hacked through the hull of the pirate craft. The sound of splashing-churning water came from the surface as a feeding frenzy lasted only a minute.

Within a few more days, the gypsies had reached the mild estuaries of northern Australia, rich with saltwater crocodile, a ceremonial delicacy.

Mohammed Algenib was indeed a handsome man, and at this time, he was in his midfifties. His features had grown more rugged than what had appeared in earlier photos. In one photo, taken in his late twenties, he could have been mistaken for a young Omar Sharif, but the mysteries of HIV were weaving Mohammed a different fate.

I met him in the hotel lobby, only days before my silently planned departure from Hong Kong. He was sitting in a lounge chair in the sunshine of the atrium. He looked up as though he'd been waiting for me. He no doubt had seen me when I'd left the elevator.

With a quiet effort, he rose from his chair. His complexion had taken an almost matte-like pallor, and his cheeks were sunken. This seemed to have happened within weeks.

"Have a drink with me." He held his hand toward the lounge.

I glanced at my watch. "I—"

"Yes," he said, "time is growing short."

What did he mean by that? His time was growing short? He knew of my plan to leave? Or was my arrest imminent?

At this time of day, the lounge was usually empty. Mohammed drew a chair out from the table to seat himself. He wore a camel-colored blazer with brass buttons and a lapel pin of the Union Jack. I waited until he was seated.

"You collected a great deal of information," he said. He had mentioned this in the past to remind me that my story was incomplete, inaccurate. "Your sources are varied. But how reliable are they?"

I didn't know where this was going.

"Everyone sees things differently," he said. "It's human nature. What you see in the mirror isn't what others see."

He motioned to a waiter near the bar. A moment later the young man appeared with a menu. Mohammed looked at it briefly and then ordered cognac. Was he no longer concerned about mixing medication and alcohol?

When the young man looked at me, I ordered the same.

"Pamela told you I killed Johnathan Allyson, and I did." He said this with such ease it was chilling. "You're under the impression that Tziporah ordered it. She did and she didn't. I followed Meyer's instruction."

"She did and *she didn't?*"

He heard my question, but he paid no attention to it.

"Allyson was the reason Meyer was denied English citizenship. Lord Firth was behind that. He paid Allyson to pursue it and then leaked stories of Allyson's dealings with the Saudis. Undisclosed dealings. Illegal arms. Weaponry. Allyson was a defeated man. He faced disgrace—possibly prison. He threatened to reveal everything for immunity. That would have destroyed Meyer. Not to mention Lord Firth.

"Nigel didn't like Meyer. Meyer represented everything that is changing in England—it was becoming so *un-British*. And he saw Meyer as a threat to Copperthwaite Mining & Mineral.

"Neither man had a complete picture of the other. Half-truths, lies, deception, paranoia. It all started to unravel. It created shadows where there were none. That's about the time you arrived. Your intellect and your eagerness to leave the factory-room floor made you dangerous."

Algenib finished his drink, and without being asked, the waiter brought another one in a fresh glass.

"It's very simple, Nicholas. We all act out of self-interest." He looked at me. "Mostly you."

"Why tell me these stories?"

"To give you a better understanding…of what you started." He looked at the cognac in his glass and swirled it. "Alcohol," he said, "is full of false hope."

My finances in the Construction Bank of China appeared to be secure. I had contacted Heinrich Eichmann, and he assured me everything was in order. My investments were now spread among several European institutions. I also withdrew several thousand dollars in Australian currency. Looking ahead, I had no idea how I'd get from Australia to Europe without a passport, but one step at a time. I felt certain that if I remained in Hong Kong, my arrest was certain.

The night before I was to leave, I stayed with Layonna at her apartment. She had taken a few of my things—toiletries and clothes—to her father's boat, along with hers. We were to depart the estuary by midmorning the next day. She was to arrive on her motor scooter at the Dragonfly Towers, and we would leave together.

That night the sky was clear. A cool breeze from the north had swept away the clouds and humidity and left a night so pure it seemed I could feel the deep-velvet indigo of space on my fingertips. I needed only to reach up and touch between the stars.

We sat on the futon in Layonna's apartment and stared at the night sky through her open window. She shivered and pulled close to me, her cheek against my chest. I kissed the top of her head, her hair perfumed with magnolia. She nestled closer, reached her lips to my neck. She nibbled sweetly. My breathing slipped. With my arm around her, I slid my hand down her side to her hip, my hand over the smooth curve. She caught her breath and pushed closer to me.

We lay back on the futon. The scent of her breath, her skin…I loved her so deeply it hurt.

I left Layonna's in the early morning. The night was still deep indigo, and the moon had slipped to the west. I saw an all-night taxi and hailed it.

The doorman at the Dragonfly Towers opened the door for me as I approached. My shirt was wrinkled, my hair uncombed, and I noticed one shoe was unlaced. The doorman gave a slight bow and smiled politely as I stepped through the door he held open.

Once inside my suite, I stood in front of the window, the glass wall, and looked out at the harbor. It was 3:00 a.m., but the moon was still bright. There was no need to turn on a light. It was against my better judgment, but I poured a glass of vodka and swallowed a couple of muscle relaxers. I lay back on the sofa and stared out at the harbor. Within minutes I felt the tingling of the carisoprodol. I thought of Adrienne. Her memory seemed far back in time, like a photograph with curled edges. Tears filled my eyes. A man has no choice in the life he's given, and his choices aren't his own, but knowing this changes nothing. I wiped my eyes. Minutes later I slipped into sleep.

I heard ringing. *Am I dreaming? Am I on an airplane hearing a fire alarm?* I forced my eyes open. It was daylight. The ringing continued. Where was it coming from? My thoughts were foggy…ringing,

ringing. I looked to the writing desk next to the wall. The phone. The landline. I sat up too fast; the room seemed to spin. I paused with my hands and arms on the sofa to steady my weight.

Ringing…ringing.

Goddamn it, shut up!…Maybe it's Layonna.

I tried to get to my feet. *What's taking so long? Why can't I stand?*

Then I was in front of the desk, reaching for the phone, picking up the receiver. "Hello?"

"Nicholas, good morning."

"Tziporah?"

"Go to your front window…The cord will reach. Look down below."

I walked to the glass wall. There was no traffic, nothing.

"Tziporah…?

"Be patient, Nicholas. Keep watching."

I looked back to the street below; Layonna appeared on her motor scooter. She came to a slow stop as someone motioned to her. She looked forward, but the person who had her attention was still out of my view. Then he appeared. Mohammed Algenib. He walked toward Layonna. He wore a dark vest over a white shirt. The vest was bulky, oversize.

Within a moment—a second, two seconds—the explosion filled the sky, billowing flames; mushroomed, purple smoke; parts of the motor scooter and body parts scattered on the concrete.

I stared. *What happened? What is this?* My mind went from one denial to another as my knees buckled, and I slowly dropped to the floor, my hands pressed to the glass.

No, it's not true! It didn't happen…It didn't…Oh God, no!

The phone had dropped from my hand and lay on the floor. I heard Tziporah.

"Tell me, Nicholas—how does it feel?"

PROGENY

Days later—or maybe less; I don't remember—Pamela was at my door. She rang and knocked and knocked and rang and knocked and knocked, until I finally answered. As I pulled the door open, she was startled at the sight of me. "What happened?"

She was without makeup, and her eyes were red.

"What do you want, Pamela?"

She stepped past me into the foyer. "You smell like vomit."

"*What* do you want?"

She started to speak, but her voice cracked. She tried again. "My mother…She's dead."

"Dead?"

"No note," she said. "Nothing."

A few more days passed, but I'm not sure. Maybe it was more, or maybe it was less—I'd lost track. The front desk had sent word they were holding a package for me. It had arrived a few days earlier—I think that's what they said.

It had been days since I had showered or had eaten anything reasonable. I increased the hot water until my scalp tingled. I thought of the sweet unconsciousness of carisoprodol and vodka. I stepped from the steamy shower and wiped the mirror clear. Beads of water ran down the glass. I looked gaunt and pale. Standing naked in the kitchen, I poured my last glass of wine and put the empty bottle back in the refrigerator. The wine took the sour taste from my mouth. On an empty stomach, it also, as Mohammed Algenib had said, gave false courage. As I left the kitchen, my foot hit the empty carisoprodol bottle on the tile floor. It rolled away.

Once I was dressed, I took the elevator down to the lobby to get my package. On the way to the elevator, I passed Algenib's old room. It was sealed off, still under investigation. But they would find nothing. The motivation—the story behind the bombing—would remain speculation for years.

As I rode the elevator down, I watched the lobby rise up to meet me. Beyond the lobby, at the entrance to the circular drive, there was no trace left of the explosion. Everything appeared normal: traffic, pedestrians, a motor scooter passing out front. At the concierge's desk, I asked about the package and was handed a tan envelope with the regional emblem of Hong Kong in the corner, along with my name, Nicholas Firthwhile, across the front. I opened the clasp on the envelope and removed my passport. There was nothing else in the envelope.

I saw Pamela across the lobby. She stepped through a shaft of sunlight as she came toward me. The blond streaks in her hair had been highlighted. She wore a blue dress with a high waist, drawn snugly beneath her breasts, as though she were beginning to show. She stopped at the desk. The grief I had seen earlier in her face was gone.

"I'm seeing to a few details," she said. "Uncle Meyer's body is in Egypt. That's where I've sent Mother." She looked at me. "How are you feeling?"

"Fine. You look nice, Pamela."

"Thank you. I've talked to my father. He's meeting me in Scotland."

I nodded.

"I don't know what happened, Nicky. Maybe you'll tell me someday, or maybe you won't. But this baby is yours, and I want you in my life. But only if you choose to be with me. And not out of pity."

"I'll see you in Scotland, Pamela."

"You know the address, don't you?"

I nodded.

"You have a history with my family...I see that now."

"I'll meet you in Scotland. But there's something I must do first."

She kissed me lightly on the lips and then pulled back to look at me. "I'm sorry for your loss," she said.

I flew from Hong Kong to Mumbai, India, and from there I had a connecting flight to Durban, South Africa. The house was near La Lucia and had been built in the early 1900s. It was Victorian and made of stone, with a red-tile roof, and had thirty-two rooms, servants' quarters, and two cottages beyond the rose gardens. The roses were divided by color: red, yellow, pink, white, and variegated. The air was perfumed with their beautiful scent. Beyond the roses were the orchards and the vineyard.

Near the house was a water garden with lily pads and blossoms of lavender and white. Fancy goldfish moved lazily through the clear water between the lilies, and birds landed on the thick pads to pick insects from the water. At sunset the light was soft pink, as though you were in an imagined paradise.

Adrienne was in a lounge chair beneath a tree. She wore a loose-fitting sundress and a sunbonnet. There was a glass of beer on the end table and a cigarette burning in the ashtray. She removed her sunglasses to better see who was coming across the yard. She squinted for a moment and then said, "Nicky, is that you?"

"Hello, Adrienne."

She got to her feet, a little shaky at first. She held a hanky to her mouth and coughed into it and then pushed the hanky into her pocket and came toward me. She looked worn and tired, and she had lost a great deal of weight. The cords in her neck were visible. It was painful to see; she was once so strikingly beautiful.

"You're still smoking!" I smiled to soften the comment.

She held me close in her arms and started to cry. "I'm so glad you're alive." She wiped her eyes and held me out from her. "You've lost weight. And your hair, all that gray. But you wear it well," she added with kindness.

Somewhere in the distance, out of sight, I heard a tennis ball strike a racket, and voices.

"Graham," she said. "He's quite grown up, you know. And engaged. A German girl, Nadine. A sweetheart."

She led me to the patio, where a native servant brought a decanter of sherry and glasses on a silver tray and set it on the table. She reached for her hanky, turned her head and coughed into it, the cigarette in her other hand. She noticed me staring at her.

"I'm going to America, you know. Some place in Texas. Houston, I think. A little touch of cancer. Nothing serious." She coughed again. "Maybe they'll give me Demerol—one can hope."

"How long, Adrienne...?"

She avoided looking at me. "I don't know," she said, her eyes looking toward the ground. "Six months maybe."

"Does Graham know?"

She shook her head. "He couldn't take it. He's not that strong."

"You have to tell him."

"Yes, I know...Nadine can do that better than I can."

Across the yard I saw a young couple coming toward the patio. They were in tennis whites, and they were both blond. Graham's blue eyes stood out like bits of sky. Nadine's features were smooth, her eyes brown. She leaned toward Graham to say something. He pointed toward me with his tennis racket. As he came closer, he appeared embarrassed.

I went up to him and hugged him close. He squeezed me.

"I thought maybe you were dead."

"No, son. I'm fine."

"Mom isn't."

For a moment there was silence. Looking at Adrienne he said, "I'm going with you."

"We both are," Nadine said. She sat next to Adrienne and covered her hand with hers. Adrienne smiled at her. The smile was filled with pain and gratitude.

I spent several days with them. My future daughter-in-law was kind and insightful. She came from a lower-middle-class family in a small town in Germany. She had been working as a nanny in Durban when she and Graham had met. She accepted Graham's wealth with an easy stride. It made no difference to her, rich or poor.

⊷⊶

After several radiation treatments for lung cancer, Adrienne died in Houston. Her body was flown to Great Britain, where she was buried next to her father.

Graham, in the years to come, would fight bouts of drug and alcohol abuse, as Adrienne had her whole life. But Nadine was there: his nurse, mentor, and lover; they never had any children.

Graham and Nadine still live in South Africa and maintain a residence in London. But I haven't seen them in years.

When I arrived in Scotland, there was a cool mist in the air with limited visibility. Once we were on the ground, the fog grew much thicker and dense. You could almost feel it in your lungs, heavy. The taxi driver cleared the windshield with the wipers and leaned forward to see through the thickness. The castle appeared as a hazy silhouette in the distance.

The circular drive in front of the castle was made of crushed stone. You could hear the weight of the taxi roll over the drive.

"'Ee ye ar', gov'nor." He set the hand brake and got out to take my bags to the door.

When I'd paid him, he started to make change, but I stopped him and said, "Thank you. That's fine."

"Obliged, gov'nor." He touched his hat.

Before I could lift the knocker, the door opened. A woman with iron-gray hair welcomed me in. Once I was through the entryway, I saw Pamela at the end of the foyer. She wore a white dress, floor length, and a blue scarf with a diamond pin. As I walked toward her, she held her hand out to me. She took my hand and pressed my open palm to her cheek. Her smile was warm. She kissed my palm.

"I'm glad to see you," she said, taking me by the arm. "Come with me. There's someone I want you to meet." She stopped and looked at me. "But you already know him, don't you?"

John didn't express any surprise when I entered the library. There was a small smile at the corner of his mouth, but that was all. I don't believe he knew I had killed Meyer. Or maybe he did. He was an astute man. He was awarded the Nobel Prize for an equation he'd developed through his study of quantum entanglement. A community of biophysicists and chemists applied his equation to their work in morphogenesis, which provided a mathematical model for the existence of life through the simple mixing of a few chemicals. When John was informed of this, he said, "Well…I never considered that."

Pamela gave birth to our daughter in late autumn. The leaves had turned and were blown from the trees; the gardener raked and then burned them out beyond the vineyard. I saw the smoke rise above the vines. To the west, dark clouds had gathered, moved inland, and then cleared. Autumn sunlight came through the tall windows of the nursery, the same room Pamela had slept in as an infant and as a child.

Pamela's love of motherhood was warm and sincere. Before our daughter's birth, we'd never discussed names, but now, as the tiny infant lay wrapped in a blanket in the curl of Pamela's arm, she said, "I've thought of a name." When she said this, she was looking at the infant, gently pushing the blanket from her tiny face with her finger. She looked up at me. "I'm going to name her after my mother."

Pamela refused the idea of a nanny or nurse, and when it was time for school, our daughter was sent to a day school, to arrive home each afternoon.

The idea of calling my daughter Tziporah was difficult at first, but that changed. She often would seek me out, find me in the library, and come running to me with a picture book to show me illustrations of fairies and sylph-like mermaids with wings. She'd crawl onto my lap and nestle against me as though I were her sanctuary, and when she was frightened at night, she'd run to our room and crawl into bed on my side.

By the age of five, she'd go through Pamela's dresser, through her lingerie, and ask what this was and that was, trying pieces on, developing her own costumes and eventually her own style. She soon discovered Pamela's makeup and was delighted. Pamela indulged her with patient love as I waited for this butterfly to emerge from the cocoon. I imagined a monarch with beautifully spread wings, yellow and gold against a field of black.

By the age of ten, she was drawn to school plays and then to the theater. Her fascination was endless with the stories and characters she invented and acted out. She studied and rehearsed on her own for months in anticipation of an audition for the lead part in her senior play. When the director named Tziporah for the lead, she seemed to emerge from her cocoon in radiant color and beauty. At this time she greatly resembled her grandmother. Her hair was black; her skin not exactly olive, but neither was it white, while her eyes were dark crystal with flecks of green.

One afternoon she came to the library to put on a dress rehearsal, to recite a few lines from *Cleopatra*. She wore a silky white dress, closely fit to her waist with a blue sash, the hem to her knees, and was barefoot. She wore a gold-colored headband with the head of serpent at the center. Her eyes were heavily made up with eyeliner, as well as eye shadow of an iridescent green, like the wings of a dragonfly.

She held the hem of her dress out to the sides and curtsied and then recited:

"Fool! Don't you see now that I could have poisoned you a hundred times had I been able to live without you?"

She then stepped back and curtsied again. Her arms were now in a pirouette as she stepped through a shaft of sunlight near the window, and—for an instant—I glimpsed her grandmother placing her bare arm in the glass terrarium with the black mamba.

ABOUT THE AUTHOR

 **J. W. Nicholas** is a student of history and also a private pilot. He divides his time among his native city of Detroit, Kansas City, and Texas.

www.ingramcontent.com/pod-product-compliance
Lightning Source LLC
Chambersburg PA
CBHW030920120626
46554CB00001B/211